SOUL SHIFTER

BY ANDJELKO NAPIJALO

Cover by Olga Cornacchia

Published by Red Boat Publishing LLC
https://www.facebook.com/Andjelko-Napijalo-110975970729073

Library of Congress: 2020918719
ISBN: 978-1-7356985-1-9

Contents

PROLOGUE

The Cathedral of Souls protruded from the central square with its jaw-dropping beauty, towering above every other building by more than half its size. A cascading, rainbow-patterned rooftop covered its impressive façade, which was decorated with carvings of major events in Thalian history.

For many centuries since its inception, the cathedral was home to the souls of those who lived sinless lives. After death, all souls moved on to the Soul Commune to be sorted. The sinless were taken to the cathedral to remain in the living realm, while the sinful were taken to the Fields of Sorrow.

Today, however, the Cathedral of Souls was a venue for a different kind of event. Once every seventy-five moons, when the sun and moon switched places in the sky above Thalia, and when fields and meadows turned into frozen wastelands, a ceremony was held at the cathedral to choose the next soul shifter.

Communal priests, dressed in long, purple robes, ornate with symbols of ancient Thalia, carried glass cages toward the cathedral. The glass cages were filled with blue particles, each representing a soul of a sinless. As the priests entered the holy place, hundreds of royals, followed by common folk, streamed into the cathedral through two large gates, eager to witness history in the making.

When the hall was full, eight large bells announced the beginning of the ceremony. The sound of the metal hitting metal traveled to the farthest reaches of the capital, reminding its citizens of this important event.

As the ringing traveled above the rooftops of the capital, a dark speck appeared in the sky, quickly moving downward. Moments later, the dark speck turned into a beautiful, dark-winged horse with two diamond-patterned horns. A long mane, forming a thick ponytail, ran down its spine. On its muscular back sat a woman dressed in black, with a dragon mask covering her face.

The horse landed gracefully at the entrance of the cathedral. The Grand Witch of Thalia disembarked the animal and entered the holy site. The royal guard pushed the restless crowd backward, making space for the most important guest of the day.

The Grand Witch approached the altar at the end of the large open hall. She reached into her tunic and pulled out a small, decorative box. The box emanated a blue glow as she placed it on top of a satin pillow. She opened the lid, revealing a beautiful, shiny bracelet depicting seven animals: a bat, a butterfly, a fox, a dragon, a bear, an eagle, and a mouse.

"Bring the prospects," the Grand Witch announced, turning toward the royal family who stood on a step above the altar.

With a nod, the queen walked over to a man dressed in a fine tweed suit, who was guarding a baby carriage.

"Sir Edgar, would you please?" the queen said. She stretched her arms toward the carriage.

Edgar pushed the carriage toward the queen. Within, her nine-month-old baby girl started crying.

The queen looked down at her youngest daughter and placed the palm of her left hand on top of the child's chest until the crying subsided. She then walked to the altar and arranged the carriage next to it.

The queen's oldest daughter, Prima, who had just turned sixteen, walked over to the other side of the altar, her eyes focused on the shiny bracelet five feet away from her.

An eerie silence overtook the cathedral hall while the subtle humming of the Grand Witch resonated throughout it.

The Grand Witch chanted for several minutes until the bracelet rose from the box and hovered above the altar. The bracelet circled around the two sisters until it stopped abruptly above the baby carriage. It then moved downward until it landed on the little girl's right wrist, immediately fusing with her skin.

Everyone inside the cathedral gasped.

The blue swarm of sinless souls formed a cloud above the little girl and descended toward her fidgety body. The girl jerked upward as the souls entered her body through her nose, ears, and mouth.

As she stiffened, her older sister clenched her fists, eyes focused on the spectacle on the other side of the altar.

Moments later, the blue cloud left the girl's body and flew toward the Grand Witch, encircling her in a blue vortex.

Several moments later, the Grand Witch opened her eyes, and the souls retreated toward the top of the grand hall. The Grand Witch turned toward the silent crowd, removing the mask from her face.

"The souls of the sinless have spoken," the Grand Witch announced. "Princess Elan is the next soul shifter."

CHAPTER 1

Sixteen Years Later . . .

With legs on the verge of collapse, Sofia fled through the dark forest. Heavy, cold raindrops pounded her pale, frightened face. Moisture and frost devoured her bare feet as they sunk deeper and deeper into the layers of cypress needles on the forest floor. The cold gripped her, making her body stiff and her legs harder to move.

She knew she was making too much noise—a product of her shallow breathing. Sofia did not know, however, where she was and who she was running from.

The last thing she remembered was falling asleep in her home, the last house on Willow Drive, in a small coastal town in Maine. She'd been watching a rerun of her favorite TV show.

When she'd woken up, she'd found herself in a cabin, apparently deep in unfamiliar woods.

Her gut had told her to run for the safety of the outdoors. She had done so, only to find herself in an even bigger predicament.

As her cold feet took her deeper into the unknown, she stumbled into a town. A town unlike any she'd ever seen.

Every building was four stories tall and connected like Siamese twins. Their tilted roofs, with crooked chimneys, had thick, gray smoke above them that kept the town moonless. The streets were made of cobblestones, which were clearly an afterthought because none of the stones fit perfectly, and they all appeared to be of different lengths and sizes.

She hadn't been there long when a nicely-dressed couple walked by her, their eyes focused on her right arm.

"It's her!" the man yelled, waving his hands. He ran toward two soldiers standing on the opposite side of the street, dressed in black and red uniforms, wearing shiny red helmets on their heads.

"Look at her right wrist," the man had said to the soldiers, pointing toward Sofia.

Sofia had looked down for the first time since she left the cabin. She wore a white nightgown that stretched down to her ankles. The lower portion of the gown was covered in mud and cypress needles. Her long blond hair was loose, freely resting below her shoulders.

Something on her right wrist caught her attention, something that did not belong there. It resembled a bracelet glowing in the darkness of the night. It was no more than two inches wide. Sofia had not felt its weight when she had been running.

It was as if the bracelet had always been there, an integral part of her. The design was intricate and unique. Even though she could not see all the details, she recognized some of the shapes—a bear, an eagle, and a fox. *It's beautiful.*

Sofia looked toward the soldiers, who started to pull their rifles from their shoulders.

"Go get her!" one of the soldiers yelled.

Sofia's heart pounded against her chest as she turned into a dark alley and started running. She ran through the streets and alleys of the unknown town, followed by the constant yelling of the chasing soldiers. After several excruciating minutes, Sofia found herself in the woods again.

Peering into the darkness, she could barely make out the outlines of trees in front of her. Still, she kept pushing forward, shuddering at the sounds chasing her.

Stop and think. Remember what Dad used to say when he faced a deadly threat at work? Take a deep breath, and clear your thoughts.

Sofia took a deep breath. The surge of fresh oxygen hit her brain, and her head started spinning. Sofia stumbled forward, and then she found herself on her knees.

She listened carefully to her surroundings, trying to determine if she was still being chased. The contours of the trees and bushes were now more distinguishable than moments earlier. Nothing moved.

She glanced above her head, where a half-moon proudly stood, a small portion of its glowing surface covered by passing clouds. The rain had finally stopped.

Voices echoed in the distance. She could not decipher what the voices were saying, but the sound of snapping branches was a good indication that they were closing in.

With more resolve, she pushed forward into the unknown. She was not ready to give up the fight yet. Her legs were heavy and slow.

Sofia kept telling herself that she was asleep in her bed, curled up at the moment, which prevented her from moving faster. Soon, she would wake up, and everything would be fine.

By now, Sofia had fully adapted to the darkness, and she could easily distinguish trees and bushes. The sound of crushing branches under her feet intensified with each stride she took, and now Sofia could make out the words from the voices.

“Quick. She can’t be too far.”

“Don’t let her slip away.”

Sofia’s fear kicked into a higher gear. She came to a stop in front of a tall fence, so tall that even the most skilled climbers would have difficulty scaling it.

Sofia’s eyes widened at the sound of her pursuers getting closer. They were not alone. They had dogs with them, vicious-sounding dogs. She could almost feel their canine teeth penetrating her soft skin.

The noise her heart was making was so loud that she thought her pursuers could hear it. It was so strong that it canceled out the men’s yelling and the barking of their hounds in the distance.

She was panicking again.

Sofia ran along the fence, jumping over fallen branches, clumsily avoiding falls. The voices were getting closer and closer. Her mouth was dry, and her hands trembled uncontrollably. She wished she would wake up from this nightmare, but the fear was too real.

“There is nowhere to go,” Sofia mumbled to herself. She was like a mouse cordoned off by a gang of cats that were closing in for the kill.

As her mind gave up the fight, her legs unconsciously continued to move her forward. Then a single jerking motion backward caused Sofia to lose her footing. She was in free-fall but did not hit the ground. Something held her suspended in the air, like magic, until she tasted a cold, salty hand covering her mouth and nose. She was unable to scream or even breathe.

One memory took hold of her mind at that moment. Images of people in dark suits flashed before her eyes. Into her home they'd come, cold and serious and unconvincingly mournful. Her dad had gone on a mission in the jungle of Colombia, they'd said. An undercover mission. And they'd lost contact with him.

Now, a boy's voice whispered into her ear, "Stay quiet. I'm here to help you."

Sofia nodded, mumbling incoherently.

The boy released Sofia from his grasp, and she quickly retreated from him, creating a void of several feet between them. A tall, olive-skinned boy with long wavy hair placed his index finger over his mouth, signaling to Sofia to stay quiet.

"Please, don't be afraid. I'm here to protect you," the boy whispered.

"What . . .? What is this place? Where am I? Who are you?" Sofia said as she ever so slightly moved two steps backward toward the fence.

"This is not the place and time to have this conversation," the boy said. "Right now, you must know that I'm here to help you. My name is Roderick. I am the man tasked to keep you alive."

"How do I know you are not one of them?" Sofia pointed toward the dissipating sounds of barking hounds.

"You do not," Roderick said. "If you come with me to the safe house, there is someone who can explain everything to you, down to the smallest detail." Roderick made several slow steps forward. "I can see on your face that you don't trust me and that you are frightened. But, deep down, you know I mean you no harm."

Sofia shifted her head slightly toward the vastness of the forest.

"I…I am confused," she replied.

"Of course you are," Roderick said. He extended his arm toward her. "Please, we must go now. Soon, you will get answers to all of your questions, I promise."

CHAPTER 2

Roderick and Sofia ran through the woods, backtracking their way toward the town. Sofia had many questions dancing through her mind. Still, she could not utter a single word due to her struggle to breathe. Roderick's heavy jacket kept Sofia warm, yet it also weighed her down, slowing her pace. When they reached the outskirts of the town, Roderick veered to the left, staying hidden within the darkness of the woods.

Daylight was creeping into the woods as they approached the wooden cabin that seemed to materialize out of thin air. It was wedged within a group of trees that skillfully concealed its whereabouts from any curious traveler. There were no other structures around. Sofia could see no signs of life coming from inside the cabin, nor did she see anything suggesting that someone lived there. That was until the smell of firewood reached her nose. She looked above the cabin, where ghostly smoke trickled out of the chimney.

The cabin's several windows were closed with heavy, wooden shutters that did not allow light to enter or escape. Sofia tried to move forward, but her feet stopped her from going any further. She stared at the cabin as her lip started trembling. *It's my family cabin. What is happening?*

Sofia loved going camping with her parents every summer. Her family owned a cabin on the shores of Rainbow Lake near Millinocket, Maine. The cabin was similar to the one she was standing in front of now. As a matter of fact, it looked identical. However, the trees surrounding her family cabin were different, mostly spruce, pine, and birch.

Roderick came to an abrupt stop in front of the cabin door and rested the left side of his face against it. A moment later, he knocked, using a pattern that he was clearly familiar with—one quick knock, a pause, three knocks in quick succession, another pause, two quick knocks, a half-pause, finished by a loud bang of his clenched fist.

Sofia focused on the door in front of her, cementing her feet to the ground and raising her arms to chest level. Miraculously, the door opened from the inside, revealing a dim light in its wake. With shoulders high, Roderick walked into the cabin as he motioned for Sofia to follow, yet she hesitated. She turned around and looked at the dark woods behind her, then back at the cabin. The cabin looked more inviting at the moment.

Sofia met Roderick's eyes, looking for a glimpse of trustworthiness in them. Something about his eyes calmed her down in an instant. Sofia forced her feet to move, quickly entering the cabin that she had earlier abandoned in a hurry.

Roderick looked once behind Sofia, in the direction of the woods, before closing the door and locking it.

****

The cabin was lifeless and desperately needed a homey touch. The interior walls were constructed out of wooden planks, possibly cedar, layered horizontally on top of each other. The eastern wall of the cabin held a round mirror, so dirty it could barely make a reflection. The southern wall held an old clock with three arms, proudly displayed on its old wooden base. The clock ticked, but the arms did not move. They were stuck at 1:38:25 p.m.

The southeastern corner of the cabin contained a small but powerful stove that radiated warmth throughout the cabin. A chimney stretched from the top of the stove to the ceiling and beyond. Next to the stove stood an old sewing machine. Layers of women's clothes sat in a pile next to it. There was a table and four chairs in the middle of the room and a single bed on the western wall of the cabin. The bed stood out from the rest of the furniture; it was large and glamorous, with fluffy bedding and intricate carvings covering the head and the baseboard.

Another door was located on the opposite side of the bed. This door bore no locks, indicating that it was not used to enter or exit the cabin. Sofia quickly calculated her escape strategy in case the situation she found herself in went sideways.

The layout of the cabin was identical to that of her family cabin on the shores of Rainbow Lake. She already knew what was behind the other door—a small room with two beds, one for her and one for her mother. Her dad always slept in the big room, as they used to call it, giving her and her mom some privacy.

Sofia felt as if she were in a dream. She half expected to hear another set of knocking passcode, revealing her father walking into the cabin to greet her.

Sofia's eyes returned to the table in the middle of the cabin where an old man sat alone. He plastered a warm, welcoming grin on his face. "Please, have a seat," the man spoke, pointing at an empty chair to his left.

"What is this? Where am I?" Sofia demanded as she retreated toward the front door. She grappled with the fact that everything felt so real. *What's happening to me?* She moved backward until her back hit the wall.

The old man stood up, turning toward Sofia. "My name is Edgar Fry." The man graciously bowed as far as his old body would allow him. Then he motioned with his right hand, directing Sofia to one of the beat-up chairs in the middle of the cabin. "Please, take a seat, and don't be afraid. We mean you no harm." Edgar pointed at Roderick. "Based on your expression, I can sense that you are frightened and seek answers to many questions that must be troubling you. I am willing to give you all the answers, but I prefer to do that sitting rather than standing." Edgar smiled as he found his way back into the chair.

Sofia inched her way toward the closest chair. Without losing sight of Roderick and Edgar, she sat down. All three sat there for a minute in silence, exchanging glances and reading each other's faces.

"Let's break this awkward silence, shall we?" Edgar spoke cheerfully. "Before I start my rambling, I want you to know that none of this will make any sense at first. But, if you stay with me through my storytelling, I promise that it will in the end."

Sofia stared at the man, still convinced that this was an elaborate dream. However, her gut was telling her that something was amiss. She could not pinpoint what, though.

Edgar repositioned his old body as he slid the chair closer to the table. He placed his rheumatic elbows on the edge of the table, interlacing the fingers on both of his hands before he dove into the story.

CHAPTER 3

Edgar appeared to be in his early eighties. His manner seemed educated, polite, and good-hearted. His sunken eyes seemed to have witnessed many things—some good, some bad, some terrible.

Sofia sat across the table from him, carefully watching his facial expressions and soaking in every word he spoke so fervently.

"I will tell you the story from the very beginning. Again, none of this will make any sense at first. I ask for your attention and open-mindedness." Edgar cleared his throat.

"Sixteen years ago, the kingdom of Thalia fell under the spell of a dark magic brought to life by Queen Prima. The magic I talk about is an ancient creation of the sacred council of the witches of Thalia.

"Witches understood the dangers of creating such magical power, but in their assessment, the positives outweighed the negatives. To create light, or good magic, they had to create dark, or bad magic, to counter it. According to their ancient proverb, 'good is evil as evil is good.' In other words, good and evil cannot exist without one another.

"The Grand Witch hid the sources used to create the magic. She separated and hid them at different locations, ensuring they would not fall in the wrong hands. She was the only person who knew where the magical sources were hidden; at least, she thought she did."

Sofia soaked in Edgar's words. Her mind kept telling her she was dreaming, that she was about to wake up and forget everything. And yet, her emotions felt real, and there was no denying the pain in her legs from all the running that she had endured, nor her battered feet from running barefoot. The pounding of her heart was also too real to be ignored. It even skipped a beat or two. The sounds of her pursuers and the dogs barking still resonated in her ears.

This can't be a dream. But what else could it be?

"The magic was created as an extension of the witches' connection to nature and all living things," Edgar continued. "Only one living person can ever control the light magic, and only one living person can ever control its dark counterpart. To further protect their investment, the witches made it impossible for just anyone to control the magic. This privilege was reserved for royals only, but not just for any royals.

"To control the light magic, the person must be a female of royal blood and possess a pure heart, free of immorality and sin. However, the dark magic could only be used by a royal tainted with negative and evil traits rooted deep within themselves," Edgar said, wiping the sweat accumulated on his forehead.

"Despite the Grand Witch's efforts," Edgar continued, "the dark magic was discovered by Queen Prima, which she then used to bring the kingdom to its knees and under her full, unquestionable control. What makes this even stranger is that no one knows why and how Prima turned so evil and how she obtained the sources of dark magic. Some talked about treason in the witches' ranks; some talked about an ancient prophecy as the reason. But one thing was certain: there were no indications during Prima's upbringing that she would turn to be an embodiment of evil."

Somehow, despite its strangeness, the story sounded more familiar to Sofia than she'd expected. "So where is the Grand Witch now?" Sofia asked. "Couldn't she just defeat Prima since she created the magic in the first place?"

Edgar nodded at Sofia's question before his Adam's apple raised high up, almost touching his chin.

"Witches create magic but cannot destroy it," Edgar said. "The Grand Witch died protecting the secret. She sensed that her end was nearing, so she shared her secrets with me—the only person she trusted to keep sources of light magic safe.

"The Grand Witch was a stubborn woman but not a traitor. She knew about my secret and did not wish to put another burden on me. It still bothers me to this day that I could not convince her to stay."

Sofia's attention switched to the bracelet on her right wrist, which she examined more closely. It was beautiful and intricate, yet simple in its design. It contained designs of several animals—a dragon, a fox, a butterfly, a bat, an eagle, a mouse, and a bear—together forming a circle.

Sofia ran her fingertips over the surface of the bracelet, which was semi-warm to the touch. Once again, the feeling of touching the bracelet seemed real; there was no denying it. It was as real as the two people sitting next to her in a cabin that looked like her family cabin on Rainbow Lake.

Her attention shifted again to Edgar as his hands trembled on top of the table.

"The Grand Witch disclosed to me the three locations which the bearer of the Bracelet of Life must visit to acquire the sources of light magic. Bearers are also known as the soul shifters by the common folk. This name is used when a bearer uses magic to transform their soul into animal form," Edgar explained.

Sofia could not tell if Edgar was grimacing or if it was simply his wrinkles overlapping each other. One thing was certain; he wanted to make sure she retained every word that came out of his mouth.

"What are these magic sources?" Sofia asked.

"They are the magic paper, the blueprint, and the Knife of Life," Edgar answered.

"The Knife of Life," Sofia repeated.

"Yes. The Knife of Life is used to cut the magic paper to specific dimensions, according to the blueprint. This process works the same for both light and dark magic. When the paper creatures are created, they must be placed into the palm of a hand on which the bracelet is worn to bring the paper creatures to life. The bearer of the bracelet can then control the creatures with their mind, breathe air through their lungs, see through their eyes, hear through their ears, and use their limbs or wings to walk or fly. They could summon and change any of the creatures on their bracelet.

"Queen Prima's Bracelet of Death contains a dragon, a basilisk, a gargoyle, a Dyoclon, a griffin, a spider, and a harpy—all representatives of evil and darkness. Your bracelet, however, appears to be less impressive when it comes to the creatures' sheer power. But that alone does not determine the victor. The victor will be the one who learns to use their powers intelligently and efficiently."

"Me, the soul shifter?" Sofia exclaimed as she pushed off from her wobbly chair and got back up on her feet. "I'm sorry, but I think you got the wrong person."

"I understand your confusion," Edgar said, looking up at Sofia. "I told you that I expected your open-mindedness with this. It is hard to process all of this at once, especially if you have no knowledge or recollection of any of it."

"It's more complicated than that," Sofia replied, her eyes shifting toward Roderick. "You…I don't know you. I don't know where I am, and most importantly…" Sofia stopped abruptly.

"Why am I even arguing with people in my dream?" She grabbed her head and accidentally pulled several strands of hair. She screamed, looking down at the chunk of blonde hair in her hands. "How can I feel pain?"

"Please have a seat," Edgar asked calmly. "It might help if I explain everything to you."

Sofia reluctantly reached for her chair. "Sorry," she mumbled. "Please continue."

"When Prima acquired the Bracelet of Death and all the magic sources, she used the creatures of darkness to conquer, kill, and enslave the people of this kingdom and beyond. The only way to combat her powers is to bring light magic to life. Remember, the light and dark magic counter each other. One can defeat the other, but this solely depends on the soul shifter's mental strength and intuition.

"Prima's powers are strong, and she's learned how to control dark magic effectively. She has a sixteen-year head start over you. It takes time to be able to fully control magic," Edgar explained.

"What I learned from the Grand Witch is that, at the beginning, the soul shifter must learn how to use the powers of the magical creatures one at a time. As the soul shifter's power increases, they might be able to control multiple creatures at one given time. It is important to understand that the soul shifter stays paralyzed in their body as they transform into their animal form. With time, the soul shifter might learn to control both and be able to be in both forms simultaneously."

"So, how do you defeat this queen?" Sofia asked, frowning.

"The only way to defeat the queen would be to destroy the paper creatures and the magic paper in her possession or by using thallium," Edgar said. "Without those things, the queen would be unable to use her magic, despite the Knife of Death or the bracelet itself.

"When you learn to control the paper creatures, you open yourself to many dangers. If one of your paper creatures is ever defeated, then it will dissolve into dust and your soul will return to your human body. If you use up all of your paper, and your last paper creature dies while under your control, you will die with it." Edgar said, slowly placing his palms on the table in front of him.

"What is thallium?" Sofia asked.

"Thallium is a precious metal found only in our kingdom and its satellite states. One small piece of thallium can burn for moons and can power various objects, including weapons. Thallium is as soft as gold, but it possesses chemical properties to bond with other living and nonliving things. You would only need a small piece of thallium to do the work. The queen's army controls all thallium mines and supplies, and it is hard to impossible to get ahold of it these days unless you are rich, loyal to the queen, or a thief. Whoever controls thallium supplies has the upper hand in this fight," Edgar said, looking down at Sofia's bracelet.

"Your bracelet is a mixture of gold and thallium, personally designed by the Grand Witch herself."

Sofia's gaze returned to the bracelet on her wrist. "What stops the queen from producing more paper and more evil creatures?"

"That is an excellent question," Edgar said. "Witches grew a single tree on the island of Porfios centuries ago. Once it grew to the right size, they cut the tree down and created magic paper out of it. Paper was made in limited quantities."

Sofia shook her head, confused by all the information presented in this short conversation.

"So, only this special paper can make magic?" Sofia asked.

"Correct," Edgar said. "Magic paper is so valuable that when Queen Prima seized the throne, she made a royal decree prohibiting anyone in the kingdom from possessing any paper or paper products. Possession of paper is punishable by death."

"Let's say I buy all of this as real. What am I really against?"

A strained smile came upon Edgar's face. "An unimaginable power," Edgar replied. "I witnessed the power of dark magic firsthand. I witnessed horrors caused by the creatures of darkness under the control of Queen Prima. They burned people alive in their homes and villages. To this day, I can hear their screams, unable to fight back. I witnessed villages and towns burned to the ground, people killed and enslaved. This is our new reality in the kingdom that once was the most peaceful of all."

Sofia stared at Edgar's watery eyes. She could see pain in them. If any of this was real—*which it is not, of course*—this kingdom was at the mercy of a lunatic queen, a queen who enjoyed killing and torturing her citizens.

Edgar looked at Sofia with glistening eyes. "Every seventy-five moons, the sun and the moon shift their positions in the sky, causing drastic changes to the kingdom. Places that were once tropical turn into frozen wastelands, and vice versa.

"At that time, the branding ceremony takes place at the Cathedral of Souls in the kingdom's capital. This is the day when the Bracelet of Life chooses the next soul shifter. We had several generations of no soul shifters because none of the prospects were female."

Edgar cleared his throat. "Sixteen years ago, during the last ceremony, two sisters competed for the privilege to become the new soul shifter: Prima, the older daughter of King Par and Queen Rhoda, and her younger sister, Elan.

"The Bracelet of Life chose the younger sister, who was still in a baby carriage. Her selection was confirmed by the souls of the sinless and the Grand Witch herself."

Sofia's mouth dropped open as she stared at Edgar. "Elan? That's the name I gave myself when I was a kid. This is all crazy. I am sorry, but I think it's time for this dream to end." Sofia was now almost positive that she was in a dream. *There are too many coincidences here.*

Edgar looked at Sofia, offering her a weathered smile. "You woke up from a coma in which you spent the last sixteen years. Your memories must be of your dreams," Edgar said.

"That's nonsense," Sofia fired back. "My name is Sofia Pride, and I'm from Maine. My parents are Jessica and Kent

Pride. We have a cabin just like this, except for this decor and the two of you. I know I'm dreaming this, and I will soon wake up in my bed and return to my old, boring life."

"Princess," Edgar said soothingly, "sixteen years in a coma can do strange things to the human body. I can tell you, with certainty, that you are not from this land you call Maine. I have been with you every day for the last sixteen years. You are the bearer of the Bracelet of Life and the rightful heir to the throne of Thalia. Your destiny is here, with us. You are the savior of the kingdom, and we have patiently waited for your return. I never doubted you would come back to us."

"No!" Sofia replied. "That's impossible. How is it possible that I speak normally if I fell into a coma as a small child? How do you explain that?"

Edgar's eye twitched as he looked directly at Sofia. "The Grand Witch cast a spell on you while she was here, delivering her secrets. The spell kept you breathing without any external help and fully fed and hydrated. The Bracelet of Life grew in size as you grew. Without the spell, you would be nothing but bones and dust. Every year, I sew a new outfit to fit you the day you wake up."

Sofia's eyes welled with tears, but out of defiance, none of them fell.

You know you are dreaming, Sofia kept reminding herself. *This can't be real.* She pinched her left forearm in protest and then jerked in the chair from the pain. *Ouch, that hurt.* Sofia growled to herself.

"Before Prima and her followers killed your father, he entrusted me with you, to take you to a safe place, away from the capital. He did not want to know where I was taking you, so Prima could not extract that information from him.

"I was King Par's most trusted envoy. He consulted me on many different matters concerning the running of the kingdom. I was his most loyal subject.

"We escaped the capital via a secret passage connecting the royal castle with the town below. Once we escaped, we took a ship to a remote area of the kingdom with vast stretches of mountains. Queen Prima found out where we went after interrogating the ship's captain who, against our wishes, returned to the capital right after he dropped us off." Edgar took a long breath.

"Prima used the Bracelet of Death to send Dyoclon to hunt us down and execute us, the same way she executed the rest of her family. I tried to protect you, Princess, with all I had. However, Dyoclon found us and managed to cut your face, inflicting damage to your brain and sending you into a coma from which you have finally woken up."

CHAPTER 4

Sofia stared at Edgar in disbelief, unable to speak. She remembered the moment of unimaginable pain and fear that she had experienced as a three-year-old and touched her face, feeling the scar under her fingertips. She could remember the event as if it had happened yesterday.

She had been in the woods with her father, collecting maple syrup, when he had asked her to stay put while he climbed a tree to get the syrup from a spot out of his reach. Sofia had wandered off into the woods.

At first, she knew where her father was, but moments later, every tree looked identical. Step after step, she had made wrong choices and moved farther away from her father.

She had picked up a branch from the forest floor and hit the leaves on the ground, revealing dark soil beneath them. Then a growl nearby caught her attention. She'd tilted her head to the left and found herself staring at a wolf several feet away from her, with his snout curled upward. His snarl had revealed his large white teeth, sharpened to perfection.

Sofia had frozen in place, yet her right arm had come up involuntarily. She'd swung the wooden stick at the wolf, which leaped forward, knocking Sofia to the ground. His heavy paws had concealed sharp claws that he swept across Sofia's face, leaving three identically spaced streaks of blood in their wake. Sofia had screamed in terror.

She remembered watching the wolf's face grow bigger and bigger as he moved closer and closer when a sudden loud *bang* echoed through the woods, knocking the wolf off his feet and off Sofia. The motionless wolf had landed on the forest floor next to her.

Her father picked her up and ran through the woods toward their cabin, her face numb. She remembered trying to soothe the numbness, but all she had found was a pool of blood that fully covered her small palm. Sofia never looked the same after that day.

"Princess," Edgar spoke, bringing Sofia back from her thoughts. "I know this is not easy to comprehend. Look at the bracelet on your wrist. The bracelet can only come off in two different ways—if you die or if your hand is severed. This bracelet is real. I am real. Roderick is real. You are real. I should have known that this would have some undesirable effect on you."

"Undesirable effect?" Sofia frowned. "You just told me that the life I knew was a dream. This means that my parents, my school, my memories, all of it were one big, elaborate dream. How would you feel about that?"

"I understand your frustration and skepticism. I do not want to pour more fuel on the fire, but I must continue my story. We are running out of time. The royal guard is searching every corner of these woods for you, and they will inevitably find this cabin. The sooner I finish, the sooner you will be gone."

"Gone? Where?" Sofia demanded.

"You and Roderick must embark on a journey to recover the sources of light magic. This is our only chance to save the kingdom. You are our only chance for survival."

Sofia frowned. Again, she mentally dismissed Edgar's words, but she did not protest listening to the rest of the story.

"The first place you must visit is the island of Cratos, where you will obtain the Knife of Life. The knife is hidden in a cave somewhere in the middle of the island, in a place where no one dares to look for it.

"The second source is located in the Castle of Madness, a small volcanic island in the middle of the Acid Sea. This is where you must find the magic paper. The Grand Witch told me that the Castle of Madness is full of mirrors that will play tricks on you. The paper is hidden behind one mirror that must be broken to reveal the paper. Breaking the wrong mirror would destroy them all and send millions of glass particles into the air, killing everyone in its path. The Grand Witch said that you must find your true self in one of the mirrors to unlock its secret."

Edgar reached into his coat pocket and pulled out a handkerchief to wipe his cheeks and forehead dry. "I am sorry for being so emotional, but it is hard to explain my excitement and concern at the same time.

"The third item is the blueprint, which is located in the City of Bones on one of the floating islands of Atmosfera. You must follow the bones of ancients which will lead you straight to the blueprints. Once you collect all these sources, you will travel to the capital to meet with my old friend, Bartholomeu, if he is still alive. Bartholomeu is a blacksmith who has a tiny shop in the lower city. He will instruct you on how to get to the secret passage that leads to the queen's castle. The passage is hidden inside an old schoolhouse in the lower city. The house looks like any other around it, so you will need more detailed instructions once you get there. So many things have probably changed in the capital since I left, so it would not be wise for me to draw a map. The queen knows you are alive and will do anything and everything to stop you from fulfilling your destiny." Edgar cleared his throat.

"Why was the Grand Witch so cryptic about these sources? If she trusted you, why didn't she tell you exactly where they are and how to get them?"

"The Grand Witch did not wish to share all details on how to obtain these items for two different reasons. The first reason was her fear that someone would find me and extract that information from me. Not because she did not trust me but because of human nature to surrender to pressure. The second, more important reason, was that only the pure soul shifter must find a way to the relics and to acquire them without outside help by conquering their own fears, emotions, and by trusting others."

Despite Sofia's resolve to stick to her guns on this one, the scary thing was that Edgar had some valid points and had answers to all her questions so far. *Is it possible that I dreamed of everything from my past? My parents, friends, home, the scar? Is it possible that my life thus far was nothing but one big lie that my subconscious told itself?*

Sofia took a deep breath and found a place of inner quiet. She needed to think about this in a rational and simplistic way, uninfluenced by her raging emotions. This is where Sofia drew a line between real and imaginary, between what made sense and what did not.

Her rage, anger, and defiance were products of her wish that all of this was just one big, elaborate dream. That would be an easy way out of this situation. On the other hand, her physical pain, emotions, and tactile senses were all products of what she was experiencing at the moment. Those actually felt real, regardless of the fact that she wished they were imaginary.

Sofia looked Edgar in his eyes, then turned her gaze toward Roderick, who was seated at the edge of his seat with his knees raised high and both legs shaking uncontrollably. Sofia closed her eyes just to open them up after two seconds. She was greeted with the same exact sight—two men seated across the table from her, looking at her with utmost interest.

"I need both of you to rest for several hours while I watch guard," Edgar mumbled from across the table. "You need to leave for Tarin before the next sunset. You must hire a captain and find a boat. I will give you a bag of gold with the promise of more. Most of the captains hang out in a pub called the Bullseye. I will leave it to Roderick to pick the right captain.

"Roderick makes good decisions, and you can trust him with your life. He's trained his entire life to be your protector," Edgar declared before he pushed himself from the table and onto his feet. "It is good to have you back, Princess," Edgar said, leaving the cabin to take watch.

****

Sofia woke up, not at first realizing she had slept more than twelve hours, way past the next sunset. She could hear Roderick and Edgar speaking excitedly outside the cabin, but she could not make out their words.

She took the time to get dressed in the clothes that she found on a chair near her bed. Everything fit her perfectly. Then she walked into the other room. It had two made beds and a little toilet room to the side of it. *My God, it looks just like our family cabin.* She had expected to have woken up by now and continued living her boring life as Sofia; but oddly, she was still here.

This is crazy. Sofia grabbed her hair with both hands and slowly pulled it. "It still hurts," she murmured

She regrouped her thoughts as she washed her face with the water sitting in a pitcher next to a handmade sink. Then she combed her hair and exited the cabin, joining Roderick and Edgar.

They stopped talking the moment she approached them and humbly bowed.

"Please stop with that nonsense," Sofia spoke, grimacing. "This is not right. I can't explain how or why, but I know it's not right."

"Only time can erase your suspicion," Edgar said.

Sofia sighed deeply and lifted her chin to look at the sky. A fresh breeze washed her face of the layers of emotional dirt that had accumulated over the past day or two. As hard as it was to believe, all she had now was this place, something tangible that she could touch and feel. Everything else felt like a distant memory.

Since the disappearance of her father, Sofia had struggled tremendously to keep her sanity in check. She understood that her life had changed in its core and that everything from that point on would fall on her mother's shoulders. Her grades had gone into a steady decline, she had distanced herself from friends, and she had fallen into a depression. Sofia craved solitude.

All the positive thoughts that had endlessly flowed through her young mind like wild rivers had become distant memories.

Her attitude reached its lowest level since the beginning of her teenage years, and her negative mood had quickly overpowered the last remnants of the old Sofia. It had ripped her apart, as if another person had become trapped inside her body . . . but there was no solution to get that person out. She had been put on medication for depression and anxiety to ease her troubling thoughts. At times, she knew that the meds were making her angrier and more miserable.

Now, faced with this new reality that clearly was not going away, despite her wishes, Sofia started to ease her stance. *Why would I want to go back to my old life, anyway? I would just be my old, miserable self with nothing to look forward to.*

Sofia looked down at her wrist, still displaying her new, beautiful bracelet. It shone and glittered. *You really are magical.* She touched the bracelet with her fingers. *Sofia the soul shifter. Sofia the Princess of Thalia. It's very catchy, I have to admit.*

"Princess," Edgar spoke. "One mistake while cutting the magic paper will dissipate the paper into nothingness. You must cut it precisely by the lines of the fold. If there is no paper left, there is no Thalia and all of this was for nothing."

"I'll keep that in mind," Sofia said, nodding.

She understood that for the time being her place was in Thalia, with Roderick and Edgar. Sofia needed to embark on a journey to find the truth about herself and to uncover the secrets behind her current situation. After all, she had always dreamed of helping others as Elan the Righteous, and now she actually had a chance to realize her dream.

"I understand that you are conflicted between what you know to be real and what you heard me say," Edgar said. "Either way, you do know that your life is in danger. If you believe you are in a dream right now, then you know the royal guard wants you dead. I suggest that you take this seriously. That is the best I can offer at this moment. I also suggest that we use the name Sofia on your travels to keep your identity secret. We do not want to draw unnecessary attention to your existence." With that, Edgar handed a purple velvet bag to Roderick.

****

Deep within the capital, Queen Prima had received news of the sighting of a girl wearing the Bracelet of Life.

Since she had decimated all her enemies—family, friends, and other loyalists—within a month during the royal purge, her life had turned into pure boredom. Queen Prima had dreamed of this day when a challenge would force her to use her dark magic on an entirely new level . . . as if she needed a reason to use it in the first place. She used dark magic often to reinstall fear and obedience in her subordinates.

The news of the girl with the bracelet gave Prima exactly what she was looking for—a chance to finish the job.

It did not take long before a plethora of mercenaries, pirates, and assassins arrived at the capital to receive instructions from their queen. The following morning, the streets were filled with wanted posters bearing images of Sofia. The offer for Sofia's head was one thousand gold coins and a small piece of thallium. That much money would last a family of four more than ten moons' worth of taxes, food, and even some entertainment. The textile posters with Sofia's face indicated in bold lettering that she must be brought to the capital, dead or alive . . . double the money if someone brought her alive!

A multitude of pirate and mercenary ships alike scrambled to leave the harbor to find the most wanted person in the kingdom.

A smile popped up on the queen's face as she stared at the poster of Sofia in her hands.

Her eyes slid down until her sight zeroed in on her wrist, where the Bracelet of Death glowed in the darkness of the great hall. Prima's heart pumped poisoned blood through her infested veins. Shadows of the dark creatures from her bracelet materialized behind her. "It's time to finish the job once and for all," Prima said, and the roar of the creatures filled the hall.

CHAPTER 5

Sofia and Roderick left the cabin behind and headed toward Tarin. Sofia wore a black tunic with pockets embroidered with gold. The hood of the tunic lay flat against her shoulder blades. Her new pair of tight, black leather pants and knee-high black leather boots squeaked as she tried to break them in.

Sofia glanced over at Roderick's clenched jaw. "Is everything okay?" Sofia asked.

"O-Of course, Princess," Roderick stuttered.

"That's not really a convincing answer," Sofia replied, meeting Roderick's ever-shifting eyes.

Roderick coughed and looked away from Sofia's intense gaze. "The last twenty-four hours have been like a nightmare for me," Roderick said as he pushed the hair away from his forehead. "I've trained and waited for this moment for many long moons. When it finally happened, it caught me by surprise. That's all. I'm upset with myself that I almost failed you."

Sofia gave Roderick a compassionate smile. "Trust me; I get it. I think I'm still living through a nightmare as we speak, so I know how you must feel. I wouldn't worry too much about it. I'm not worth all the trouble I've caused so far."

Roderick simply smiled in response.

"Tell me about this dream of yours," Roderick asked, shifting the topic away from himself.

Sofia found his question to be a perfect segue into reality . . . or what she had thought was her reality. She talked for minutes while Roderick listened attentively. He drank up all the information Sofia threw at him.

Roderick learned about the place called the United States of America, about burgers, coffee, ice cream, video games, cars, and airplanes.

"Roderick," Sofia said, "there is one thing Edgar did not mention when he was telling his story." She met his eyes. "He never told me about you. How did you end up with him, and what brought you here?"

Roderick lowered his head. "My father was the commander in the royal guard during your parents' rule. He swore to protect the kingdom from all enemies, internal and external. When Queen Prima started the coup, he saw that the end to the kingdom that he had sworn to protect was all but certain, so he facilitated your escape with Master Fry. They went their separate ways but agreed on one thing—to keep you alive at all costs. They managed to stay in touch with the help of the Grand Witch," Roderick said.

"What brought me here was my father's dying wish to fight Prima's terror." Roderick's voice began to crack. "I'm sorry. I get emotional when I remember my father."

"It's okay," Sofia replied. "I am sorry for bringing it up in the first place."

"Please don't be," Roderick said.

The next ten minutes passed in total silence as they traversed the woods on their way to Tarin.

Before they reached the town, Roderick explained his plan to Sofia. "When we get downtown, we must go straight to the Bullseye pub, where we need to find a captain for hire who can take us to Cratos. It's imperative you stay silent and do not, under any circumstance, show the bracelet to anyone. If someone sees it, they will know who you are and that will be the end of our journey . . . the end of us. I also suggest you cover your face with something so they don't recognize you."

Sofia nodded at Roderick as they strolled into Tarin.

****

When they arrived at the center of the town, they were greeted by the sight of hundreds of flags bearing royal crests hanging from almost every building. The flags displayed a black dragon with a sword in one claw, clasping a fortress with the other as he stood on it. The crest represented Queen Prima's tight grip over the kingdom and all its inhabitants.

Not too far ahead of them, several large ships were docked at the harbor that bustled with life. Street merchants were selling elixirs, fish of all sorts, hats, gloves, and many other random things. Slaves wore heavy, clawlike shackles around their ankles, loading large wooden crates onto one of the ships as the royal guardsmen closely watched. *A lot of people for such a small town.*

As they neared the harbor, Sofia's mouth dropped open. She stared at three large ships floating in the air. They were almost identical in size, but they all bore different flags.

Sofia focused on one in particular. The ship had a large propeller on its stern and odd-looking sails that resembled oversized umbrellas. It looked like nothing she had ever seen before. It had futuristic contours but was made mostly out of wood. The umbrella sails stretched like a canopy above the captain's quarters of the ship.

"Floating ships? Really?"

"Not just floating—flying," Roderick explained. "I assume you have never seen ships like these in your dreams?" Roderick asked. "Remember when Master Fry mentioned thallium? Well, this is thallium at its best. Our ships run on it. Even my bow is made out of it," Roderick explained.

Impressed, Sofia shifted her attention to the large crates that the slaves were loading onto the ship. She wanted to ask more questions but figured the less she knew, the better. She did not want to get invested in this whole charade.

As they made a right turn onto one of the side streets, avoiding several horse wagons with more crates to be loaded, Sofia and Roderick found themselves walking straight into four royal guards walking toward them.

Sofia's mouth dried in an instant. She tried to swallow, but there was nothing to swallow. Tunnel vision kicked in, and instead of staring at the road ahead, she stared at the eyes of one of the soldiers. His eyes pierced through Sofia's hood, reaching her eyes. She fought hard to keep her eyes closed so he would not be able to penetrate them. She prayed for a safe passage, but before she was able to finish her prayer, the soldier spoke up.

"Hey!" he yelled as the other three stopped in unison.

Sofia and Roderick stumbled.

"Hey, I'm talking to you two! Where do you think you are going?" the soldier asked.

Sofia peered from under her hood, keeping her gaze fixated on the cobblestones in front of her.

"What are you two younglings doing out here at this time of night?" the soldier asked.

Sofia was trying to think of a clever answer when Roderick jumped in. "I'm taking my sister to our aunt's place to take care of her. She is very sick. I didn't want to let her walk by herself on these filthy streets."

The soldier gave Roderick an intense stare and then looked at Sofia. "Is she a mute?"

"No, she's not, sir. Just shy."

Another soldier jumped into the conversation. "Shy? Just like our poor little Barton likes them. Aren't you upset that no mothers want to let their daughters hang out with you, Barton?"

"Or to mention your name," another soldier added. The other soldiers burst out laughing.

"Not funny," the soldier named Barton said, still staring at Sofia.

"Let the kids be, Barton. We have better things to do," one of the other soldiers said as they continued to walk toward the harbor.

"Take off your hood," the soldier demanded as he repositioned himself to get a better look at Sofia.

Roderick leisurely shifted his hand near his waist, reaching for a small blade hidden under his jacket.

Sofia froze, feeling like running but unable to because her legs were locked in place.

"I hate repeating myself. Take off your hood," the soldier demanded.

Sofia lifted her left arm and slid the hood off her head, revealing her frightened face to the soldier.

He studied her for a moment in disgust. “That scar. Don’t I know you from somewhere?”

“I don’t believe you do, sir,” Sofia spoke, her hands trembling.

“Hmm. You look familiar, but I can’t place where from. I better not catch you out this late at night around these parts, or you will have other things to worry about besides your sick aunt.”

“Yes, sir,” Sofia answered as she pulled the hood back up to conceal her face.

The soldier once more looked at Sofia suspiciously. “I think I’ll be seeing you again,” the soldier said as he shifted his duty belt, laden with two pairs of hand shackles and a midsize blade. The soldier threw one last long stare at Sofia before he continued walking, reuniting with his comrades.

CHAPTER 6

Roderick and Sofia stood in front of the old, rundown Bullseye pub. There was nothing appealing to it, at least not on the outside. It would be the last place Sofia would ever go to if she were to visit Tarin as a tourist. According to Roderick, though, it was the best place to hire a captain.

"If you need anything, you can find it here. If you have enough gold or thallium to pay for it, that is." He repositioned his short blade, which protruded from under his jacket, making sure it stayed concealed. "Are you ready?"

"As ready as one could be under the circumstances," Sofia replied, adjusting the hood on her head.

Roderick pushed open the pub door. The pub's décor was born of hundreds of moons' worth of illegal trading deals made under its tables, blood spilled after games of cards, and alcohol consumed on its premises. The loud atmosphere inside the pub was a byproduct of the consumption of too much alcohol by its patrons. The smell of alcohol was overpowering, making Sofia gag.

Thirty-something pairs of eyes pierced through Roderick and Sofia as they stepped in.

They dragged their feet through the center aisle, trying to act natural. Out of the two empty tables available, Roderick chose the one farther away from the bar. It gave them a better vantage point to see who arrived and who left the pub.

As long minutes passed, the intensity of the looks gradually ceased. The pub's patrons returned to gulping alcohol, playing cards, and making all sorts of illegal deals.

The bartender yelled at Roderick and Sofia from across the counter, warning them that they had to order something or get lost.

"Two glasses of water, please!" Roderick yelled back at the bartender.

Silence fell hard in the pub. Every pair of eyes turned toward them at once. Sofia looked at Roderick, who blushed. The silence stretched until, finally, the crowd erupted in a frenzy of laughter.

Sofia could not believe how many different ways people could laugh. From the screech of a skinny man sitting adjacent to their table to barking laughter from a burly man sitting at the bar. Their response surprised Sofia, who caught herself kicking Roderick in his left shin under the table. She did not want to do it, but it was too late to control her instinct.

Roderick flinched and looked at Sofia. "What was that all about?"

"Water, really?" Sofia mocked. "So much for fitting in with the crowd."

Roderick pursed his mouth. "Sorry, that was the first thing that came to mind. You wanted me to order alcohol?" he argued.

That's a good point. As if I would do a better job of fitting in?

Their short interaction was interrupted when the bartender brought two glasses of clear liquid and placed them on the table, spilling some of their contents. “There’s your water,” the bartender said as he walked away to return to whatever he was doing before.

Sofia’s upper lip pulled up into her wrinkled nose when she picked up her glass of water, not because she was about to drink water from a questionable source but because the glass was disgustingly dirty. She brought it close to her nose to see if she could smell it. To her surprise, it smelled like alcohol.

Sofia looked at Roderick and protested, “This isn’t water; it’s alcohol!”

Roderick brought his glass to his nose. “You are right. It’s *karish*.”

“What’s *karish*?” Sofia asked.

“It’s a liquor made out of *Kari* fruit and cypress needle extract.”

“That sounds gross,” Sofia said. She placed the glass back on the table with no intention of drinking its contents when she noticed several men staring at her from the nearby table.

“Everyone is staring at us,” Roderick whispered. “I don’t think we have a choice but to drink this if we want to fit in with the crowd.”

Sofia grinned as she slowly moved the glass closer to her mouth. She pressed the glass to her trembling lips, forcing her mouth to allow the liquid to spill inside. She swallowed and instantaneously grimaced.

She turned her gaze to the right and noticed three burly men still staring at her. She raised her left hand, holding the glass, and the three men cheerfully grabbed their drinks and bottles and raised them to their lips, draining them to the last drop.

Roderick threw a smile at Sofia, raising his glass in the air. "That went well. Cheers."

Sofia looked at him, her face turning bright red as she professed with disgust, "That's not funny. Next time, you should take one for the team."

After her first shot of karish, Sofia watched Roderick. He constantly shifted left and right in his chair. Each minute spent inside the pub increased their chances of being discovered by the royal guard or one of the thousands of mercenaries employed by the queen to capture and kill royals and their supporters.

"Do you see anyone you could approach?" Sofia asked.

"Now that you mention it, see that man over there?" Roderick pointed at a burly man near the bar. "That is one of the living legends, Captain Ferald the Great. He is known for his voyages to places beyond the kingdom's influence. Stories say that he has encountered creatures and people beyond anyone's imagination. On his many journeys, he fought and suffered greatly but still survived against all odds. People say his voyages have come with a price in the form of many scars."

As Roderick shared the story of Ferald the Great with Sofia, she unconsciously touched her scar to make sure it was still there, a confirmation that she was still who she thought she was.

"Are you going to ask him to take us to Cratos?" Sofia asked.

"There's no point. He's out of our price range." Roderick shook his head. "But I might try approaching the guy to his left. The intricate carving on his blade indicates he might be a pirate captain as well."

As Sofia looked over at the bar, still trying to get rid of the lingering sourness of karish, she spotted a red-haired girl standing next to Ferald the Great. She was not much older than her and Roderick, and she wore form-fitting black clothes with red accents on her athletic body. A leather belt decorated with two long blades squeezed her elegant hips.

A wide smile decorated her pink face while her long fingers elegantly plucked a glass of karish from the bar. Sofia recognized a slight hint of makeup on the girl's face, but she would be flawless without it. The girl in black downed the glass, unfazed by its content. There was not a hint of disgust on her face as the liquid rolled down her throat. For some reason, Sofia was mesmerized by the girl in black.

A tattoo on her right forearm caught Sofia's eye. She could not tell what it was.

At that moment, Roderick got up from the table and approached the bar, circling the man he had earlier identified as a potential captain for hire.

Sofia shifted her focus toward the girl in black again. She stared as the girl continued to go about her business of making acquaintances and downing glasses of karish.

There was something about her body language that Sofia found interesting. The girl sized up everyone around her. Then she zeroed in on a table with several yapping men playing cards. A large grin formed on the girl's face.

The girl motioned to the bartender to give her one more glass of karish. The moment the glass reached her hand, the girl threw a silver coin at the bartender. She walked away from the bar with the glass of karish clutched in her left hand.

As she walked past the table where the four loud yappers played cards, the girl purposely entangled her right foot in a chair, spilling the glass over one man's jacket. The large, bald man grunted as he tried to clean his dirty jacket with his hands. But he only made more of a mess, smudging layers of dirt that accumulated on his checkered jacket.

The girl in black apologized to the man, but her body language did not match her words. She scrambled to clean the jacket with both hands. She even blew warm air onto the jacket's wet areas as if that would help dry it quicker.

"Move, you filthy scum!" the burly man yelled as he shoved the girl in black with one hand, pushing her back ten feet.

When the girl in black disengaged from the man's wet jacket, Sofia noticed a quick yet delicate movement of her left hand, which skillfully reached inside the man's jacket pocket. She pulled a small but bulky wallet from it. The girl in black stumbled back from the shove, and she used the momentum to insert the wallet into her jacket pocket, swiftly concealing it from the man's view.

While the bald man and his companions laughed at the girl's clumsiness, a smirk appeared on her face. Her naturally pink face brought a beautiful contrast to her dark clothes and her liquid green eyes. The girl gained full control over her body as she then headed out of the bar.

Sofia looked at Roderick to see if he had seen the interaction, but he appeared too busy looking around for a captain-for-hire in a sea of drunk, aged men.

The girl in black made her way toward the exit. After several steps in that direction, though, the wallet fell out of her jacket and onto the floor. It appeared that Sofia was the only person to see this.

As the girl in black moved past Sofia's table, Sofia stopped her by grabbing her left arm. The girl in black reached for the saber in her belt as she spun around to face the threat.

"Excuse me," Sofia said, holding the wallet. "You dropped this on your way out."

The girl blinked. Then she looked Sofia in the eyes. She released the grip on her saber and said, "I don't know what you are talking about. That's not my wallet."

Undeterred, Sofia pushed her hand closer to the girl, clutching the wallet. "It's okay," she whispered. "Take it."

The girl in black flashed an odd smile as she shifted her eyes to the left of Sofia's face. It was clear she was not paying attention to Sofia but to something behind her.

When Sofia turned around, she faced a large group of men staring at her right hand, which held the stolen wallet. Even the bald man in the checkered jacket stood there, looking at his wallet but not claiming it.

The odd silence was broken when the man who stood next to the victim of theft said, "My gods, she's wearing the Bracelet of Life!"

A glance down revealed the Bracelet of Life, flashing its full glory to everyone in the pub.

Sofia winced. *Great. I'm an idiot.*

When she turned back to the girl in black, the girl was no longer there. She caught a glimpse of the pub door rocking back and forth, indicating the girl had just left.

The front door soon disappeared in a sea of men surrounding Sofia in the middle of the pub, like a gang of sharks surrounding a single fish.

“It must be our lucky day,” one of the men said as they closed the distance, preparing themselves for the greatest catch of their lives.

Chaos erupted as two men grabbed Sofia by the arms. She kicked her legs as they carried her toward the exit. Roderick jumped into the crowd, pulling out a small blade he kept at his waist. Then, with a twist of a hand, the short blade transformed into a sword.

From the corner of her eye, Sofia saw Roderick charge her attackers. Before he could get to her, another man cut off his path and pushed him aside. Roderick lost his footing and went flying over a table, knocking down empty glasses and scattering them all over the wooden floor. He swiftly regained his footing and squared off, readying himself for another attack.

Sofia’s heart started pounding. With Roderick facing down a group of fifteen large, armed men, she feared the fight was all but lost.

Roderick raised his right arm, preparing for an attack, when the door to the pub swung open, welcoming a platoon of royal guardsmen. They pushed through the rowdy crowd and grabbed hold of Sofia.

Sofia screamed as she kicked one of the advancing soldiers. When the guardsmen managed to grab hold of her arms and tie her legs, they focused on Roderick, who still stood in the same spot with his blade clutched in his right hand. A chain-like contraption fired from one of the soldiers’ guns. It bound Roderick’s arms and chest together, forcing him to drop his blade.

A gang of guardsmen tackled Roderick to the ground as he tried to fight them off with just his head and teeth. Roderick made his last stand on the ground, topped by several heavily armored soldiers.

CHAPTER 7

Inside a bare and silent jail cell in downtown Tarin, a small hole near the top of the southern wall allowed just enough light to illuminate two prone bodies on the rough stone floor.

Sofia looked over her left shoulder at Roderick. He sat in the corner, hugging his legs with both arms while resting his forehead on top of his knees.

"Roderick, are you awake?" Sofia whispered.

Roderick mumbled something back without moving.

Sofia moved closer. "Are you okay?"

Roderick unglued his face from his knees and faced Sofia. "I'm reflecting on how we ended up here," he groaned. "I can't believe we were caught before we even started our mission. I didn't even try to save us—to save you!"

"You need to stop blaming yourself for this. It was all my doing that got us here. If I hadn't been stupid enough to try to talk to that girl, we wouldn't be having this conversation right now."

Sofia clenched her fists, wanting to punch the wall in anger.

She knew the real reason for Roderick and her being here was her naivety and stupidity. *This is not Roderick's fault. He did everything he could to keep me safe. If he'd tried fighting his way out of the pub, he would have been killed.*

Just then, three royal guards walked through the only door on the other end of the hallway. One of them dragged his metal beat-stick along the metal rods of the cell, making a frightening sound.

"Wake up, worms!" he shouted. "Today is your lucky day. Today, you'll become famous. Hundreds of people are out there, waiting to watch your performance."

"Performance?" Sofia asked.

"You poor things have no idea what's waiting for you on the outside. You're going to die today in the most painful way imaginable."

Shivers racked Sofia's body as she tried to process the guard's words. "This . . . this is all a misunderstanding," she proclaimed.

"There's no misunderstanding about your bracelet. It doesn't matter how much you try to explain yourself, that bracelet doesn't lie. We know who you are. We know what you are." The guard spat. "Preparations are underway at the central square to make sure we have a spectacle today. But don't mind my excitement. I'm here to give you a chance to give up any other collaborators in exchange for a quick, painless death."

Sofia looked in the direction of the guards, on the verge of pleading for her life. "But there are no others. We didn't—"

"That's what I thought, you filthy worm," the guard cut her off. "Have a nice death."

The guards quickly turned around and left Sofia and Roderick to themselves.

As silence filled the room, Sofia looked at Roderick, surprised he had not spoken up in their defense. "Thanks for your help," she muttered, crossing her arms.

"There was no reason to argue because your bracelet is our death sentence. It wouldn't matter if I came up with the greatest excuse imaginable. The fact that you wear the Bracelet of Life is all they care about. There are no negotiations with the royal guard."

Sofia looked at her right wrist with disgust. She hated the bracelet. She wanted to get rid of it, but she could not remove it. How could such beauty be such a curse?

Sofia grabbed the bracelet with her other hand, trying to rip it apart, but the bracelet remained in place, fused into her skin. She knew that unless she cut off her wrist, there was no way of removing the bracelet. She was the bracelet, and the bracelet was her. It did not matter if she liked it or not.

Sofia turned away from Roderick and closed her eyes. A tear or two gathered in her eyes. She wanted to let them spill out like a waterfall, but something stopped her. *Isn't this what I wanted for myself since Dad went missing? To run away from the reality. . . to die in order not to feel the pain?*

Every time Sofia dreamed of something dramatic and scary, she would wake up the moment she was supposed to die or be caught by someone or something chasing her. Countless times, she had been chased in her dreams by a variety of bad guys, and her escape was possible only if she outran them or if she woke up seconds before they laid their hands or claws on her. But this time, she wasn't waking up.

Since her father's disappearance more than two years ago, Sofia closed herself in, not allowing anyone else into her life. Not even her mother.

She looked down at Roderick, whose face was now visible in the light spilling in from the hole in the wall. It bugged her that he was in this situation because of her, regardless if this was a dream or not. He should not die because of her.

I need to come up with a plan to escape from here, with or without Roderick's help.

Sofia surveyed the jail cell for anything useful. But, other than a small roach climbing up the wall toward the hole, there was nothing. Sofia went through her clothes just in case the royal guard had missed something when they had searched her, but she came up with nothing. She had the bracelet, but what was the point if she could not remove it, let alone use it?

****

Several more hours of useless attempts to escape passed before Roderick and Sofia were dragged out of the cell, chains wrapped tightly around their wrists and ankles. Four royal guardsmen flanked them with their rifles at the ready. They were led by another guard with more medals on his uniform than Sofia had teeth. It was the same guard who had given them their eulogy several hours earlier.

When they finally reached the prison courtyard, they were momentarily blinded by the sun that shone so brightly above them. They had to close their eyes, relying on the guards to guide them.

My God, this has to be the most beautiful day ever. It's such a shame that it will also be my last. Sofia thought about the possibility of tripping and falling to the ground to buy some time. But what would be the point? It would not matter if she got a scrape or two when she was about to be executed for wearing a bracelet. *A freaking bracelet!*

As they turned the corner behind a large building, the central square came into view. The sound of chanting masses resonated through the square and beyond. There were hundreds of people, cheering and chanting, eager to witness the deaths of two people whose only crime was—

What is my crime? That I wear a stupid bracelet on my wrist?

Sofia snapped back to reality after one guard pushed her from behind.

They were paraded by their captors in front of the angry mob, guided toward a large stage in the middle of the square. Some spectators threw rocks at them, while others spat in their direction. Luckily, none of the disgusting spit found its way on Sofia's face. She was not sure if Roderick was so lucky.

Roderick and Sofia had not exchanged a single word since they had left their prison cell. What could she possibly say to a person she barely knew? Would a nice *thank you* suffice? He had saved her life in the woods, after all, and she had repaid him by throwing them in jail, followed by a grandiose execution. She stayed quiet, sure her voice was the last thing he wanted to hear right then.

They approached the wooden podium speedily constructed for their execution party. Two guards took Roderick to the other side of the stage. Several workers hammered at a contraption sitting in the middle of the podium while one of them was sharpening a large circular blade in the middle of it.

Is that a saw? Sofia stared at the large hard-toothed round object as she was led up the four steps of the podium.

A voice next to her spoke. "Ha, it's you. I told you I would be seeing you again."

Sofia's eyes met those of the soldier who had interrogated her on their way to the Bullseye the night before.

"I knew there was something about you. I knew it," the guard spoke, full of satisfaction.

Sofia ignored the bragging, trying to concentrate on her thoughts, thoughts she could hardly hear over the spectators' screams.

I wonder how many of these people came to the square of their own free will. Look at them. How can they be so happy and cheerful while watching two people go to their deaths, two people they know nothing about? Maybe that's what's expected of them.

Sofia looked back toward the huge saw in the middle of the stage, where a man played with a crank attached to a motor that operated the contraption.

A tall, dark man climbed onto the podium. His biceps were larger than Sofia's thighs, and scars zigzagged all over his bare chest. His appearance alone could give someone a heart attack. *I bet this guy feeds on people's fear.*

The two guards flanking Sofia dumped her into a wooden chair situated in the middle of the stage on one end of the saw. Leather straps were stretched around her waist and legs, followed by buckles. If she wanted to leave, the chair would have to go with her.

Roderick underwent the same shackling procedures on the other side of the saw contraption. His face showed no emotions. She could not tell if he was scared or just hiding his fear.

The crank brought the saw contraption to life. The screeching of the saw coming to life was horrific. The blade spun a million turns per second, and Sofia swore it turned into a monster made of flesh and bones.

The heavily muscled man motioned with his head to the guards to move away from the chairs. Then the sound of the spinning saw muted the sound of the cheering crowd. Sofia began to move closer toward the deathly contraption. Roderick moved toward her at the same pace.

My God, what a way to die. Cut in half by a saw!

Beads of sweat formed on Sofia's forehead, trailing down her face. The heat created by the spinning saw washed over her body as she inched closer to it.

Two feet left.

Now more than ever, she wished that this was all a dream. But, despite her fear and imminent death, she still wasn't waking up.

The screaming of the saw intensified. Sofia's entire body grew taut. She closed her eyes and clenched her teeth. She prayed not to feel the pain. She prayed for it to come and go as quickly as possible.

Bracing for the impact, Sofia screamed when the sound of the saw changed its tone. It sounded as if the saw connected with something foreign. Something in its path, perhaps? The squeaking noise of the spinning saw turned into a hum and then a squish. Yet, the pain Sofia had anticipated was absent.

As she reluctantly opened her eyes, screams swelled around her. She knew her mouth was closed, so it could not be her.

Sofia stared at the body of the bicep man. He was lying on top of the saw table with an arrow sticking out of his head.

Roderick lay on the other side, moving back and forth in his chair, trying to free himself from the restraints.

Not more than three inches away, the saw was stuck, stopped by an arrow lodged in its path. *How could a single arrow stop a saw of such size and power?*

A glance over her left shoulder revealed frantic spectators scattering in every imaginable direction. Then a flock of birds flew over her head.

Wait! Those are not birds. Those are arrows!

Finally, understanding dawned. Men in armor lay all over the wooden podium, arrows sticking out of their bodies like peacock feathers. Some guards were engaged in one-on-one combat with men who did not wear any armor. They looked like pirates. That was the best way she could describe them.

Then, something caught her eye.

The girl in black running through the crowd of soldiers, slashing one after another with two blades that she held tightly in her hands. She swung the blades flawlessly, and the men around her fell like dominos, none of them ever getting back up.

Sofia couldn't help thinking, *Did she come to finish me off for ratting her out, or did she come to save me? But why would she? She doesn't owe me anything.*

When the last royal guard fell to his death, the girl in black walked up to Sofia with such conviction that Sofia was sure she was going to kill her. When she stood two feet away, she raised the blade up. Then the blade came down, making contact with the leather straps that kept Sofia tied to the chair.

"Get up. It's time to go."

The next thing Sofia knew, she and Roderick were climbing up into a pirate ship as arrows and bullets flew and fell around them.

The girl in black and her crew scrambled to depart the harbor. Several men dragged up the anchors; some released the sails, while others secured the cargo or loaded the ship's cannons. Everyone on the ship had a job, and they knew well how to do it.

Bullets kept flying over their heads as they squatted down on the starboard. One bullet struck the wooden pole several inches above Roderick's head.

"That was close," Roderick said as he crawled his way around the ship's deck.

The ship's engines came to life, roaring like a pair of angry lions awakened from a short sleep. The sound drowned out all the others. Seconds later, the sound disappeared, leaving only a subtle humming that felt soothing.

Sofia's head started spinning. It did not take long for her to realize it was not her head spinning; it was the ship. After the spinning sensation stopped, the ship swiftly ascended into the clouds. Umbrella-shaped sails contracted up and down like a pair of lungs, sending air to the ship's heart and brain. Moments later, the ship moved toward the horizon, gaining distance from the town and the sounds of firing guns. Now the only sounds left were the humming of the ship's engines and Sofia's labored breathing.

She understood that she had cheated death once more and that she had the girl in black to thank.

CHAPTER 8

Once the ship reached safe skies, far from Tarin, Sofia and Roderick found themselves sitting on a wooden plank in the middle of the ship, staring at the horizon. Sofia expected a scolding from Roderick, but to her surprise, none came.

"Who are these people?"

"I think they are mercenaries, or thieves, or maybe both," Roderick answered. "I have never seen their flag before, so I can't be sure."

Sofia looked at him with a blank expression on her face. "Isn't that a bad thing? I thought mercenaries hunt down the royals and their supporters so they could sell them to the queen."

"True," Roderick said, pushing several stubborn bangs off his face. "I don't know what their intention is, but I'm glad they saved us from that horrifying . . . saw thing."

Sofia let a laugh escape her lips.

As her laughter faded into the fluttering of the sails, a familiar voice spoke up. "Our intention is not to hand you over to the queen . . . if that's what you are thinking." The girl in black handed Roderick his collapsible bow and two of his blades. "I believe these belong to you."

"I-I don't know what to say," he stuttered.

"Say thank you and that you will pay me a lot of gold when we finish the job."

Roderick and Sofia looked at the girl in black with a hint of suspicion.

"My name is Dalia Swiftblade," the girl offered. "*Captain* Dalia Swiftblade. And you got yourselves a captain and a ship."

"But . . . how . . .?" Roderick exclaimed.

"I overheard you trying to hire a captain at the pub. You need a captain, and I need money to keep my crew. The last thing I want is a mutiny on my ship and one of my men impaling me through the heart for not paying them on time."

"But you don't even know what our journey is and where we need to go," Roderick said.

"All I know and care about is that you have money. If you continue to inquire about what I know or intend to do, you will need way more money to convince me to take the job."

"Just one problem," Roderick said. "I lost all my gold when they caught us at the pub. I don't have any on me to give to you."

Smiling, Dalia reached into her jacket pocket and pulled out a familiar purple velvet bag. She shook the bag as the clanking of the metal coins rang from within. "I think you already paid me in advance."

Roderick looked at the bag, his eyes as wide as they could stretch. "That's my money bag?"

"Indeed," Dalia said as she returned the bag to her pocket.

All Roderick could do was extend his hand. "I guess we have a deal."

Dalia looked at his hand suspended in the air, then spun around. "I don't want your empty hand. I'll shake it when it's full of gold."

Roderick narrowed his eyes as he shouted after her, "You don't even know where we're going!"

"Island of Cratos!" Dalia yelled back as she marched toward the center of the ship.

"I don't trust her," Sofia said.

"What other options do we have?" Roderick responded.

"Why didn't she approach you at the pub to offer us the deal?"

"Your guess is as good as mine," Roderick said. "If she was willing to risk her life to free us from the queen, I don't have a reason not to trust her. Any enemy of the queen is my ally. If she is motivated only by the money, then let it be."

Sofia did not like what she was hearing, but it was hard to argue. The girl in black *had* saved their lives, despite her attitude and potential hidden agendas.

"All I ask from you is to be extra cautious when dealing with her," Sofia said. "Promise me that much."

Roderick bit his lower lip as he looked at her. "You know you can order me to do whatever you want, and I would do it. I'm here to serve you and protect you," Roderick said humbly.

Sofia was taken aback. "Thank you for that, but I would still like to call these things favors instead of orders."

****

The cool breeze coming through a small, oval window in Sofia's sleeping quarters calmed her as she drifted into a deep sleep. Her dream took her back to Maine, to a field behind her house where she used to play with Luna, her dog. Even in her dream, she was aware of her predicament.

As she threw a tennis ball for Luna to fetch, a thought entered her troubled mind. *I am dreaming in my dream. How's that even possible?*

When Luna returned, her tail wagging, full of pride in her accomplishment, a feeling of melancholy overtook her. *I miss you, Luna. I wish you could hear me right now. I wish you could be with me through these tough times.*

Luna had been her sanity, her engine of positivity. Without her and her father, things had never returned to normal.

As Sofia swung to throw the tennis ball for another round of fetch, a shrieking sound took her by surprise. She looked down to find herself standing on Luna's tail. Moments later, Sofia was staring at the ceiling on Dalia's ship, listening to the shrieking of the wooden planks above her.

Despite her exhaustion, Sofia could not relax enough to fall back asleep. So, she grabbed her tunic and walked out to the main deck of the *Sky Serpent*.

Dalia approached her as she sat. "I'm glad to see you here. I wanted to ask you something. I was wondering . . ." Dalia paused.

Sofia searched her eyes for evidence of deception but could not find any. Then again, it was Dalia's seeming innocence that had tricked her in the first place at the pub.

"Wondering about what?" Sofia asked.

"That night at the pub, when you asked me if I dropped the wallet, did you want me to get in trouble, or were you trying to be a Good Samaritan?"

"Does it really matter?" she asked.

"It does matter . . . I want to make sure I can trust you from now on, little princess," Dalia said.

Sofia looked at her, unable to speak for a moment. "How—how did you—"

"How did I know?" Dalia interrupted. "Maybe because of the bracelet you wear on your wrist. You can drop the entire incognito charade because I know what you are, little princess.

"My mother told me about a girl with the bracelet. The one that was supposed to save the kingdom. Years passed and the kingdom fell deeper and deeper under Prima's control. Our savior was nowhere to be found," Dalia said.

"Your mother is onboard?" Sofia asked.

"No."

"Then where is she?"

"My mother's dead!" Dalia barked, startling Sofia enough to jump back. Dalia took a deep breath and looked over the railing of the ship. "When I was five, my mother hid me under a bed, in a secret compartment below the floorboards of our house.

"Then she went out to confront the royal guard. She was a courageous woman.

"She put up a good fight before they shot her point blank."

Sofia gasped. "I…I'm sorry to hear that."

"They threw her body inside the house and torched it with me still hiding underneath. I remember hitting the wooden planks, trying to escape the inferno, but then, I lost consciousness."

"That's horrible!"

Dalia shrugged. Her eyes had cleared as if she'd drifted away for a minute and had just now come back to herself. Clearing her throat, Dalia began to move away, but Sofia stopped her.

"H-How did you end up as a pirate captain?"

Dalia stopped walking away. She turned back, and Sofia beheld the least guarded emotion she'd ever seen the girl in black wear—a smile. Small, maybe even tiny, but genuine.

"Well," Dalia went on, "when I finally opened my eyes, I was surrounded by pirates who gave me a new life, a reason to fight.

"I started training in the art of piracy by washing dishes and mugs on board Sir Longbow's ship, the *Black Ghost*. It didn't matter to me as long as I was flying to new places with my new family.

"By the age of ten, I was training with the rest of the pirates, mostly hand-to-hand fighting, knife throwing, and sword fighting. My skills with the sword caught the eye of Sir Longbow, who eventually took me under his wing so that he could train me personally.

"By the age of thirteen, I was going on raids with other pirates, attacking trading ships to strip them of their precious cargo. My first real kill, however, came at the age of fourteen during an attack on a rival pirate ship. Sir Longbow was killed during that raid, and things changed for me drastically.

"When Sir Clayton Bloodborne took over the ship, he marginalized me for being a girl. He kept telling me that my place was with dirty dishes, not with the sword.

"I challenged Bloodborne to a duel, which he could not refuse according to the pirate code. Everything else is history."

"That's incredible," Sofia murmured.

Dalia's smile froze on her lips. Her eyes lost the dreamy quality they'd taken on and became clear and cold again. She turned away from Sofia. "I can't believe I just shared my entire life story with a total stranger." She started to walk away again.

"I didn't want you to get in trouble at the pub!" Sofia yelled after her.

Dalia stopped mid-step and turned around. But then, a moment later, she left the deck without speaking.

Sofia had spoken the truth, but not all of it. It would take much more courage to tell Dalia that she had stopped her at the pub because she wanted to be friends and because she felt some sort of inexplicable connection to her.

After a while, Sofia returned to her sleeping quarters, which had once been the ship's pantry. She lay on her bed, staring at the ceiling and reflecting on her experiences so far. Her eyes were heavy, her mind switched off involuntarily, and she fell into a dreamless sleep.

****

Sofia's sleep was interrupted by the violent rocking of the ship. She fled her room and found Roderick in the belly of the ship. Once they made their way up to the main deck, they caught sight of a turbulent sky above them. The ship's crew frantically ran around as if they had never witnessed a storm.

Dalia appeared out of nowhere to warn Roderick and Sofia, "You two need to retreat to the safety of the lower deck. We have entered a hunting storm."

"A hunting storm?" Sofia asked.

"There are storms above the Raging Sea that are—how should I put it?—intelligent. Their sole purpose is to hunt ships that fly by. These storms have minds of their own."

As Dalia finished her explanation, the clouds above them opened up. Several silver, gelatinous drops fell on Dalia's face and arms. Her eyes widened in horror. She frantically wiped her face with the sleeve of her jacket.

"Run!" Dalia screamed. "Run below the deck and find a place to hide. Now!"

One of Dalia's crewmembers was struck by a bolt of lightning. The bolt burned through his body, leaving only death in its wake.

Roderick pushed Sofia forward. "Run!" he yelled.

As they ran toward the door leading to the ship's lower deck, several more of Dalia's crew were incinerated on the spot as the lightning struck them. Dalia was right behind them, yelling at them to move faster.

Once in the safety of the lower deck, with the ship shaking violently, Dalia turned toward Sofia and Roderick.

"Hunting storms use different ways to feed on their prey," she said.

"This one, in particular, uses metallic drops to act as a conductor when it makes contact with the human body. Lightning then targets these metallic drops, killing everyone in its path. I've seen many different hunting storms in my life, but never this one. I've only heard of it from other captains who managed to survive them. Now, I need you to stay here while I go out there and get us out of this mess."

"Wait—what?" Roderick said. "You're going out there?"

"Someone needs to if we plan on living another day." Dalia grabbed several long cloths from a nearby stand. She placed a translucent cloth over her head, covering her entire body. Then she dashed out into the storm.

Dalia went straight for the ship's helm, skittering around the holes in the main deck caused by the lightning strikes. The deck was now littered with the bodies of her dead crew.

Several raindrops hit the cloth covering Dalia's head, and she removed it, throwing it away from her. As the cloth flew toward the ground, lightning pierced through the cloth, leaving a large hole while the rest of the cloth caught on fire. "That was close," Dalia said, placing another cloth over her head.

She managed to get behind the helm of the ship and pull a lever that plunged the ship downward. The ship was now engulfed by the storm in every direction.

As she fought to keep the ship afloat, another drop hit the cloth next to her right shoulder. She worked fast to trash it, but it snagged on the blade hanging at her waist.

She managed to remove it just as the lightning struck the spot where the metallic drop had fallen moments earlier. It penetrated the loose portion of the cloth, missing her entirely.

Dalia repositioned the cloth over her head while still steering the ship in a downward spiral. The ship struggled to stay afloat, but the engines were still intact. The thunderous noise intensified, canceling out all other sounds in the area. Dalia looked up and swallowed hard.

As they plunged ever deeper, a small opening appeared in the distance, revealing a clear blue sky beyond.

Moments later, the ship penetrated the thick clouds and found itself on the opposite side, in the clear blue skies. Dalia immediately corrected the ship's course with several turns on the stern as she pushed the engines to their limits, wanting to get as far away as possible from the deadly storm that had left her ship wounded and several of her men dead.

CHAPTER 9

The next day was more promising, marked by thin clouds and a lot of sunshine.

As they cruised through thinning cloud cover, Roderick joined Sofia on the main deck.

"You look rested," Sofia commented.

Roderick looked over his left shoulder and smiled at Sofia. "Thanks. This is my face with zero hours of sleep. I couldn't close my eyes after that crazy storm yesterday."

Sofia laughed, looking into the blue sea dotted with fluffy white islands of clouds. "It's beautiful. I've never dreamed of flying on a pirate ship. It's surreal. I'm scared to say that I'm starting to like it here."

Roderick smiled. "You only needed to almost die three times to start liking this place," he joked.

They both laughed, drawing the attention of several of Dalia's crew walking by. They carried their dead comrades . . . casualties of the hunting storm.

As Sofia was about to add something, a voice from above yelled, "Land! I see the land!" It was the ship's lookout, patiently standing on top of the mast.

Roderick and Sofia looked into the vastness of the sky but could not see land.

Dalia approached them, flanked by two of her men. "It appears we have arrived at Cratos. Once we find a good spot to anchor, we'll drop you off. I plan on staying with my men to work on fixing the damage to the ship. I hope that's all right with you two."

Roderick and Sofia exchanged looks of agreement. "Make sure you return before sunset, or you might find an empty harbor. I hate to wait on people, even if they are of your creed." She disappeared as fast as she appeared.

****

The way the island of Cratos was formed and shaped gave Sofia and Roderick only one possible route to travel. From up above, the island did not look like it stretched for too long in either direction, maybe five miles in diameter. The center of the island seemed more mountainous than the rest, making the central region the prime target for their exploration.

They moved as fast as they could, not knowing how long it would take them to find the cave, and with Dalia's ultimatum in mind. They barely spoke, preserving their energy for what was to come.

About two miles into their hike, Roderick pulled two apples from his pocket he brought from the ship and handed one to Sofia. She took it without any reservation and dug her teeth into it.

“Thank you,” she said, dropping a piece of apple. Sofia bent and picked up the lost piece, blew at it, and threw it back into her mouth. “Five-second rule,” Sofia said, blushing.

Roderick offered a sheepish smile.

As they finished their fruity lunch, the two continued their walk.

Another half hour passed before they arrived at the bottom of the mountain. The terrain became more rugged and harder to hike. They moved much slower now. Some of the rocks were so smooth they were slippery.

As they pushed forward, the terrain turned into a full-blown obstacle course, forcing them to climb, slide, and squeeze to fight their way through the rocks. There were many crevasses indented on the surface of the mountain, and they all looked the same in size and shape.

They followed what appeared to be a trail through the mountain for another half hour until they reached the top. Several other peaks surrounded them, but the one Sofia and Roderick stood on appeared to be the tallest. They scanned the area around them, looking for anything different, anything worth checking further. To their disappointment, nothing stood out.

The moment reminded Sofia of her first-ever hike with her dad. At the age of eleven, she embarked on a journey to conquer Mount Katahdin, the tallest mountain in Maine. Her dad had been an avid hiker, and he wanted Sofia to experience the joy of hiking at an early age. To him, hiking was bonding with nature, devouring its beauty, enjoying the sounds and smells.

The Mount Katahdin hike had been Sofia’s entrance to the world of nature, the world her father loved and cherished until the day he disappeared. When she climbed the top of Mount Katahdin, in an instant she had shed all of the dirt of modern living that she had brought with her. Sofia could see her dad's teary eyes as he lifted her in the air to celebrate their victory.

Sofia came back from her short trip down memory lane as her eyes focused on the edge of the mountain they stood on.

"Edgar said to look at the place that no one dares to look for," Sofia said.

"What do you have in mind?" Roderick asked.

"Below us is a boulder that's sticking out of the mountainside, blocking the view of what might be below. Who says that the cave is not hidden under it, invisible from this vantage point."

"That's a good point," Roderick replied, approaching the cliff.

"The only problem is, how do we get down there?" Sofia said.

"I happen to have an answer for that." Roderick smiled as he reached for the back of his belt, pulling out a small circular object from it.

"What's that?" Sofia asked, staring at the dark object in Roderick's hand.

"It's something my father left me before he passed away, together with this belt and weapons," Roderick said, looking down at his hands. "It's a rope."

"A rope." Sofia frowned as she bent to get a better look at it. "But it's so . . . small."

"That's the beauty of thallium." Roderick pushed one end of the small object and a hook appeared. He attached the hook between two rocks and pulled on it. "This should do it."

Roderick then pushed the object on the other end, releasing another hook. He pulled on the hook and a skinny blue wire came out with it. He attached the other hook to his belt.

"Ready to test your theory?" Roderick asked, extending his arm toward Sofia.

"I hope you know what you're doing," Sofia said as she slowly approached Roderick.

"Trust me on this," Roderick said. "All you need to do is wrap yourself around my waist and I'll do the rest."

Sofia reached around and hugged Roderick, her face sitting plush against his chest. She could hear Roderick's heart ticking.

"Are you ready?" Roderick asked, looking down at the top of Sofia's head.

"Ready as one can be," she answered, her voice muted from the lips rubbing against Roderick's jacket.

"On three. One, two, three . . ."

Roderick jumped back from the cliff with Sofia tight around his waist. The wire extended as they seamlessly glided through the air.

When they cleared the bulge, a dark hole appeared before them, carved into the rock.

"Guess what?" Roderick yelled.

"What?" Sofia said, her face still glued to Roderick's chest.

"I think we found it."

Roderick released more of the wire until his feet landed on the ledge in front of the cave.

Sofia still held on to him for dear life.

Roderick took a deep breath. "You can let go of me now," he said, smiling.

Sofia released her grip, ungluing herself from Roderick. She looked past Roderick toward the dark hole in the mountainside.

"I wonder if this is the right cave," Sofia said.

"There is only one way to find out."

****

The entrance to the cave looked far from magical. However, Sofia and Roderick entered it with slight hesitation, leaving daylight behind. From there, the cave stretched deep into the mountain's belly.

Roderick reached for his belt and pulled out a flashlight operated by a dynamo motor. He pumped on a little crank on top of the flashlight in rapid succession, making the flywheel hum and instantly produce light, illuminating the cave in front of them. There was nothing but fifty feet of barren rock on either side.

As they moved forward, a weird feeling overtook Sofia—the feeling of walking straight to her death.

"How could Edgar be so confident the Grand Witch did not give up locations of the light magic to the queen?" Sofia asked, her forehead wrinkled up as she looked at Roderick.

"I don't know. I can say with certainty that Master Fry cares about us and would never send us into a trap," Roderick answered.

"What I'm worried about is what the Grand Witch did to protect the relics. I guess there is only one way to find out."

Sofia remembered Edgar saying that the bearer of the Bracelet of Life must use her intuition to find solutions to her riddles. *Easier said than done*.

They continued to trudge down the rugged, rocky floor of the cave until they approached a fork. The trail to the left glimmered with a red light, while the other trail was consumed by darkness.

"Which way do you think we should go?" Sofia asked as she moved ever so slightly toward the left.

"I think we should go left because there is something at the end of the path," Roderick answered without hesitation.

"Maybe the Grand Witch wanted people to believe this was the way. What if this is a part of the test?" Sofia had a weird feeling that everything around her was part of a test.

"Use your intuition," Roderick said as he pulled out his short blade.

Sofia looked left, right, and then back to the left. "Follow me and make sure you step where I step."

As they traversed fifty feet down the illuminated path, the humming of the flashlight stopped, and the light went out. But the path through the cave was still visible due to the constant red glow. Roderick placed the flashlight back onto his belt.

Each step was precisely measured, with Roderick stepping on the exact spots where Sofia had stepped moments earlier.

Not too far down the red path, the cave opened into a medium-sized chamber. When they reached the entrance, they could finally see from where the red light originated. In the center of the chamber, seven pedestals stood, forming a circular design. The red light illuminated the entire hall, not allowing any other color to coexist.

Seven intricate carvings decorated the walls that enclosed the hall. The hall floor appeared to be made out of metal rods, not thallium. The rods formed a checkered design reminiscent of their jail cell in Tarin.

Sofia and Roderick tested the metal rod floor for resistance, stepping on it briefly before jumping back to the safety of the rocky ground surrounding it. Once satisfied, they stepped onto the metal railing, their eyes now wholly adjusted to the red glow.

Each pedestal in the center of the room had a square metal tile with engraved animal shapes sitting on its top. A closer look revealed a butterfly, a fox, a bear, a bat, an eagle, a mouse, and a dragon, all the same size and shape. A glance at the carvings surrounding the hall revealed square-like indentations in each one of them—seven carvings, seven metal animal tiles. *I bet these things go into those holes in the wall.* Sofia continued to study them.

Curiosity got the better of Sofia, and she moved to the edge of the hall to further investigate the carvings.

Roderick spoke from behind her. "Do you think these metal things go into those slots in the carvings?"

"I believe so, but the question is: which one goes to which?" Sofia's intuition was telling her that the answers lay in the carvings prominently featured on the hall walls.

With her right hand, she gently caressed the wall in front of her, trying to connect with the carving in some way. As much as the carvings mesmerized her, she could not shake off an eerie feeling that something lay beneath her . . . deep in the mouth of the cave.

"What does your intuition tell you?" Roderick broke the silence.

"I don't think it's telling me anything but to admire the art. It's beautiful. Do you recognize any of these things?" Sofia asked.

Roderick approached Sofia and looked at the carving. "I don't think so. Some of the clothes people wear in these carvings are similar to what the soldiers in the kingdom used to wear before Prima took over. Other than that, none of the scenes or faces look familiar."

Sofia looked at Roderick. "It's odd, but I feel a connection to these carvings. It feels as if I were here when they were carved or something. I could almost feel them and see them being carved."

"That's impossible; Master Fry spent every day of the last sixteen years with you in the cabin."

"I don't mean physically," Sofia explained. "It feels as if I watched them being carved from up above as if I were a spirit or something. It's hard to explain." She shifted her attention from the carvings to the pedestals.

As she moved toward the center of the hall, something stopped her from advancing further. She shifted her head downward. There was no way of telling how deep the hole beneath them was because the darkness fully consumed it.

Sofia changed her posture as she made two more steps toward the pedestals with her attention still on the floor beneath her. She did not want to wake up a sleeping monster if one waited below them. "Roderick, can you bring your flashlight here and point it down? I want to see what's beneath the floor."

Without hesitation, Roderick took the flashlight, pumped it twice until the light materialized, and then pointed the light beam down into the dark hole. Both of their jaws dropped open.

The light revealed dozens of human skeletons. They were piled on top of each other, some fifty feet below, with long, skinny spikes protruding from their bodies. Goosebumps sprouted along Sofia's body as the skeletons' hollow eye sockets stared at her from below. Swords and bows rested next to their motionless remains.

"Are you all right?" Roderick asked.

"Yes, yes, I'm fine. I don't know what I expected to find there, but this was not it." Sofia struggled to understand what she was facing and how to put it all together. She looked at the tiles on the pedestals, then at the carvings on the walls, then at the bodies below. *How do they all fit together*?

Sofia studied the tiles the way she used to study math problems in middle school. She had to look at things from a different perspective. These objects craved her attention. They wanted her to pick them up. *There is only one way to figure this out.*

Sofia's hand trembled as she brought it close to a tile featuring a bear. Sofia grabbed a tile and slowly lifted it from the pedestal. Roderick stood fast next to her, staring at the tile in Sofia's hand. They waited for ten seconds. Nothing happened.

Sofia walked over to one of the carvings featuring the birth of a child.

Roderick stood aside, observing Sofia's every move.

She looked at the bear engraved on the tile, then extended her arm toward the hole in the wall. It was a perfect fit.

"Should I?" Sofia asked, looking over at Roderick. He just shrugged his shoulders.

Sofia pushed the tile into the hole until it clicked. The moment it did, the portion of the metal floor beneath her opened. She dropped, her hands scrambling for the edges of the floor in desperation. She missed.

And yet, she stopped falling.

She looked up to find Roderick struggling to hold on to her left arm, his face contorting in agony. Sofia looked down and could swear that the bodies below had gotten excited to have another person join them.

"Hang on! Reach out with your other hand!" Roderick yelled. He struggled to hold on to Sofia, his feet digging into the metal floor above her.

Using her last iota of strength, Sofia grabbed hold of the metal edge of the floor. With the momentum of Roderick's pull, Sofia found herself out of the death hole.

The moment Sofia cleared the opening, the metal trap door returned to its previous position, making the floor whole again. Then the tile that Sofia had placed into the carving on the wall was swallowed. Moments later, it reappeared back on the pedestal in the center of the hall.

Sofia lay on her back next to Roderick, forcing a laugh, though she did not really find it funny. "Looks like the trust-your-instinct thing is working just fine for me."

Roderick muttered something as he regained his footing and stood up. He then extended his hand toward Sofia, and she took it. He pulled her back up. "I guess we now know the bear doesn't go in that spot," Roderick said, and then they both burst out in genuine laughter.

Sofia took a deep breath. This situation, bizarre as it was, reminded her of something. Every birthday and every Christmas, Sofia had found papers left by her dad indicating that she had puzzles to solve. Solving them meant she would get a present. Despite the nuisance of it, she had loved every second of those elaborately planned games and appreciated the presents way more if she had to work for them.

She had never given up on any of her father's puzzles, and some had been really tough, way above her age level. She had no intention of cowering out of this one.

Sofia understood the importance of clearing her thoughts and concentrating on what she had in front of her. She could not make another mistake. Her action had been caused by irrationality.

I have animal shapes on metal tiles in the middle of the room. The same animals I have on my bracelet. I have trap doors that open when you put the wrong object into the wrong carving hole. Carvings . . .

Sofia stopped for a second. *I need to figure out the carvings.*

Wheels turned in Sofia's head. She concentrated on the carvings that surrounded her, circling the hall. She visited all the carvings and studied them in detail once more. The first thing she noticed, which was sort of obvious, was that the carvings did not have any correlation to her bracelet or any of the animals.

One carving depicted the birth of a child, one the death of an old man, and another of people laughing, dancing, hugging, and kissing. Yet another showcased a single warrior fighting a monster. The fifth carving showed an army surrendering to a single woman holding a flower. The sixth was of a family with ten children sitting at a dinner table full of food and wine. The last carving displayed a chaotic scene of people running in every direction as the ground below them opened up, swallowing many. In the background of the carving, a city burned.

Sofia looked at her bracelet, then looked back at the carvings and repeated the process several more times. *This doesn't make any sense.*

An idea took shape in her head. An idea about animals and their symbolism. She had learned some of them from movies, some from books, and some from school.

"My God," she exclaimed, moving closer to Roderick, who was staring at the metal tiles.

Roderick looked at Sofia with wide eyes. “Did you figure it out?”

Sofia did not want to give him false hope. “Not really, but I think I’m onto something.” She positioned herself next to Roderick so both were facing in the same direction. “Check out the first carving to the left, the one that shows the birth of a child.”

Roderick looked over.

“I think the key to the puzzle is that we need to find a connection between the animals on these squares and the carvings on the walls.”

“Not to sound rude, but I think we figured that one out from the get-go,” Roderick said, blushing.

Sofia continued her explanation. “I think we need to look at the bigger picture here. We must draw a meaning of these carvings and put them into the perspective of the animals, or what they stand for, what they symbolize.

“Check it out. I believe butterflies symbolize birth or resurrection. At least, they do in my world. So, if I’m correct, the butterfly must go into the carving symbolizing the birth of a child.”

Roderick looked at her. “Is this your intuition talking?”

“Not sure. It’s hard to explain. It just feels right,” Sofia replied. “If you look at the carving of the army surrendering to a woman with a flower, I think this depicts love . . . passion maybe?” Sofia stopped, allowing the wheels to spin inside her head. “As a matter of fact, this might symbolize wisdom or cleverness because the entire army surrendered to one person. See, foxes symbolize wisdom or cleverness.”

“Remarkable,” Roderick noted. “Please continue.”

Sofia turned a little to the right and faced the carving of a family with ten children sitting at a table filled with all sorts of meats, fruits, and drinks. “I think this carving represents abundance, fertility, or expansion, maybe. I believe a mouse symbolizes fertility. The carving of a warrior fighting a monster should represent courage or strength, which a bear is a symbol of. The man dying might represent death, and bats are symbols of death. The carving depicting people celebrating, dancing, and kissing could symbolize happiness—or humanity, maybe. An eagle symbolizes these things in my world. Lastly, the carving with the city burning and people running and dying most likely represents chaos and death, which a dragon is a symbol of. This one is tricky because bats also represent death. However, this carving has fire in it, and dragons breathe fire.”

Roderick plastered a huge smile on his face as he watched Sofia. “I think you are onto something, for sure,” he said. “If that’s your instinct talking, then you should go for it. It seems to me that you already knew the answers to all of this.”

Despite this revelation, Sofia was hesitant to act on her instinct alone. “In my mind, this all sounds right, but I don’t know if all these animals have the same symbolism here as they do back home. I can’t afford another mistake, or we both might die.”

“There is only one way to find out,” Roderick said as he motioned toward the metal tiles in the middle. “Let’s try some?”

Sofia slowly approached the pedestal and, with her shaky arm, picked up the one featuring a butterfly. She walked over to the carving depicting childbirth. Her right hand began to ache, and she realized she was squeezing the metal object hard. At the same time, she stared at the metal floor below her feet. Roderick stood aside, prepared to jump to her help if the floor suddenly gave way.

She extended her hand toward the carving. Her arms trembled uncontrollably as she pushed the butterfly into the wall. She did not hear the clicking sound, so she applied more pressure. She pushed it into the hole until she heard the familiar clicking sound.

Sofia froze in place, expecting the floor to give in, but nothing happened. She knew at that moment that she had gotten it right.

"You did it!" Roderick exclaimed, hardly able to contain his excitement.

"Let's not get ahead of ourselves," Sofia said, sweat dripping down her face.

Sofia repeated the process with the mouse. She pushed it to the carving of a family having a sumptuous dinner with ten children. Anticipation was the worst . . . waiting for that *click* and then anticipating the floor opening as a result.

The object connected to something in the carving, producing a distinctive clicking sound. The floor stood in place. *Two down . . . five to go!*

The next one was a bear. She pushed it below the carving of a warrior fighting a monster. She got another *click,* and the metal floor stayed intact. The next was the fox. Sofia pushed it below the carving of an army surrendering to the woman with the flower. She received another *click,* followed by another success. The eagle went next. It clicked into the carving of people celebrating. With each new object she placed into the carvings, Sofia's confidence grew, knowing she was on the right path.

The dragon was next. Sofia was confident she was going to get another *click.* She pushed dragon tile into the carving depicting people running from a burning city. She got another *click,* and then Sofia and Roderick stood frozen, waiting for something to happen, but nothing did.

Then the sound of working gears chased away the silence of the cave. The familiar red glow outlined the metal animal shapes, and the carvings came to life. The proud father held and kissed his newborn child. At the same time, the mother reached out to hold the father's arm. Soldiers threw down their weapons as they surrendered to the woman with the flower. A commander of the surrendering army knelt before the woman as she handed the flower to him. People were running to save their lives from the falling earth as the fire raged in the background, people dancing and celebrating. There was something beautiful about it. It was the first time Sofia had witnessed real magic.

As they were enthralled by the live display of the carvings before them, a large stone pedestal rose from the center of the hall. Sofia and Roderick slowly moved toward it, still cautious about every step, making sure this was not a part of an elaborate trap designed by the Grand Witch. To their amazement, a small knife with a blade made out of thallium appeared on the pedestal. It featured a red handle, as red as the glow in the hall, with seven animal shapes etched into it. A subtle baby blue color emanated from the knife's blade.

Sofia reached out for it, then lifted it from the pedestal, expecting the floor to give in. Still, the ground held fast, just like she and Roderick.

"It's beautiful," Sofia said as she gasped at the knife's beauty. "I never thought a knife could be so beautiful, but there is always a first time for everything."

****

As Sofia and Roderick climbed the barren rock above the cave, a pair of spying eyes watched their every move. The person returned an ocular to the pocket of a dark leather jacket, pulling out an instrument that resembled a communication device. With several precise strokes of fingers over a keyboard-like face, they sent a message.

Cave located. Got the knife.

CHAPTER 10

As the *Sky Serpent* floated through the air above the beautiful landscapes of Thalia, Sofia and Roderick sat on their favorite wooden post near the edge of the ship. They were absorbed in the beauty of the magic knife tightly clenched in Sofia's hands.

"It's magical," Sofia said as she rolled the knife in her hands.

Dalia cleared her throat as she approached. "Would you like to know more about the knife?" Dalia extended her arm toward Sofia, who handed it over.

"It is beautiful . . . just as my mother described it," Dalia said, sounding genuine. "For all these years, I thought this knife was just a legend, but now I'm holding it in my hands. If only my mother could see it."

Sofia looked at Dalia, whose eyes glistened under the midday sun.

"My mother told me stories about this knife and a princess who could control magical beings carved out of magical paper. The stories were so grand. She talked about soul shifters battling forces of evil, and they always stood victorious. It was a beautiful story. But that's all it was—a beautiful story."

Sofia held her breath as Dalia handed the Knife of Life back to her.

"I think you are wasting your time with this." Dalia smirked, then strode away.

****

Another day passed, and nothing changed on board the *Sky Serpent*. Dalia stalked around the ship, and Sofia and Roderick rested in their separate rooms, awaiting their next adventure. The winds were favorable, and they pushed the ship forward at a good pace.

Then yelling came from the ship's surface, followed by a loud *bang* and a violent jerking of the vessel. Sofia and Roderick were thrown to the floor.

Oh no!. . . Another hunting storm. Sofia ran out of her room and bumped into Roderick in the hallway.

Roderick grabbed his belt, and they both ran outside, only to be greeted by the chaos of battle between two pirate ships. The *Sky Serpent* fired relentlessly, as did the other ship. Wood and metal shrapnel knocked down men on both vessels.

Wide, wooden planks with metal claws flew from the enemy ship and onto the *Sky Serpent*. As two boats became one, attacking pirates ran over the planks, oblivious to the vast space below them. Some of them swung from heavy, long ropes, bypassing the planks altogether. Dalia was on the opposite side of the ship, slashing the intruders with her blades, not giving up a single inch of the ship to her enemy.

One sky pirate jumped from the rope behind Dalia's back. He moved through the air gracefully. It was impossible to ignore his finesse, but it was even more impossible to ignore his intention.

The pirate landed on the ship's deck some twenty feet behind Dalia. He released his grip on the rope, allowing it to return to the other ship. Then the pirate readied his machete and clenched his teeth as he ran in Dalia's direction. He raised the machete ever so slightly, preparing to issue the final blow, which would effectively end this battle. Killing the ship's captain was the ultimate prize for any pirate.

Roderick squeezed his bow, transforming it from a simple stick into a fierce weapon. He whipped out an arrowhead from his belt, which extended into a full-sized arrow with a single touch at its center. Roderick placed the arrow to his bow, clinched the tail tight to his face, stopped his breathing to level the aim, and then released his grip on the arrow. The arrow flew past two of Dalia's crewmembers before finding its target on the other side of the ship.

The arrow struck the advancing pirate through the left side of his chest, penetrating his heart. The pirate released his hold on the machete as he fell to the floor next to Dalia.

Dalia turned around at the *thump* the dead pirate made. Her eyes met Roderick's. She thanked him with a firm nod of her head, then returned her attention to two other pirates advancing her way.

As the fight escalated on the *Sky Serpent*, things became dire for the defenders. With the prospect of dying at any moment, Roderick pushed Sofia against the wall. "Stay here, and do not move," Roderick instructed her.

Roderick barely had enough time to turn before two flying pirates came at him. He avoided the collision by dodging to the right, but as he tried to regain his footing, the attacking pirates were already on top of him. Roderick fought with the long blade that he had exchanged for the bow. He was mostly defending their attacks as he moved them away from Sofia.

On the other side of the deck, Dalia was in a strategic retreat, under constant attacks by two pirates.

As Dalia moved backward, Roderick continued to deflect attacks by his attackers. With each step back, Dalia and Roderick got closer to each other without realizing it.

Moments later, Dalia and Roderick found themselves back-to-back, engaged in a conversation while fighting off constant attacks by mad pirates.

“I need to ask you a favor!” Dalia yelled.

“Doesn’t seem like a good time to ask for favors!” Roderick yelled back.

“There is only one way to win this battle. We must destroy their engines.”

“And how do you intend to do that?” Roderick asked as he defended another attack by the enemy’s saber.

“I have a bomb made out of thallium in the chest under my bed. Only thallium can destroy thallium. If I can get the bomb into the engine room, that would do it.”

“Sounds like a plan,” Roderick said. “But what is the favor you wanted to ask of me?”

“I need you to keep these pirates busy while I retrieve the bomb.”

Roderick’s answer had to wait while he struck the final blow to his stubborn enemy, slashing the bodies of two pirates with his blade. “Sure thing. I’m ready whenever you are.”

As if they’d rehearsed it, Roderick engaged Dalia’s attackers, freeing her to do what she intended.

Dalia ran toward the captain's quarters. As she got close to the door, she was blindsided by another pirate. "Watch it!" Sofia yelled, throwing herself at the advancing pirate, knocking him down. Dalia looked down at the pirate and pulled out a short knife from her waist and flung it downward, striking the pirate in the neck.

Dalia nodded at Sofia and entered the captain's quarters of the ship. She rushed into her room and, shortly after, came out with a round object that subtly glowed a baby blue color. She ran past Sofia, returning to the battle.

On the other side of the ship, Roderick had defeated two more pirate attackers and moved toward the deck door. He did not get far when a sharp object struck his right shoulder, forcing him to drop his sword. An arrow protruded from his shoulder as blood spurted out. Roderick looked up and spotted a single archer on top of the main mast.

With a quick shake of the head, Roderick bent to pick up the sword with his left hand so that he could continue the fight. However, his movement was restricted by the protruding arrow.

As Roderick struggled with the arrow in his shoulder, Dalia ran across the ship, holding a small, circular object radiating a blue color.

Dalia turned toward Roderick, zeroing in on his wounded shoulder. She stumbled over the body of one of her crewmen.

Roderick grimaced as he grabbed onto the arrow struck in his shoulder.

"Go destroy that damn ship. I'll cover you!" he yelled at Dalia.

"Are you sure about that?" Dalia asked.

"Just go!" Roderick moved against a nearby wooden crate, looking for cover.

Dalia skillfully avoided several incoming arrows fired in her direction. It appeared that the archer on the main mast had lost interest in Roderick and was solely concentrated on Dalia.

Dalia grabbed a long rope attached to a wooden pole near the center of the ship, held the thallium grenade in one hand, and ran toward the edge of the ship.

Roderick grabbed his bow. Then he looked at his wounded shoulder. He grabbed the arrow with his other hand and pulled hard on it. The blood rushed out of his shoulder like a waterfall. He squeezed his teeth and placed the bloody arrow onto his bow. He aimed the bloody arrow at the archer and released his grip. Before the archer was able to fire at Dalia, Roderick's arrow struck the archer's chest, penetrating his heart and sending his body over the railing and into the abyss below. Dalia looked over at bleeding Roderick, offering him a smile and a nod.

****

Dalia jumped off her ship in a freefall, avoiding the wooden planks connecting the two ships. The leap took Dalia farther toward the rear of the enemy ship, which housed the engine room. This was one mission that had to be executed perfectly, with no room for error. Many lives depended on her.

Dalia bypassed all the fighting above her and arrived at the portion of the enemy vessel that housed the engine room. A flash of bright light blinded her for an instant.

When she regained her senses, Dalia had already passed the engine room . . . or what was left of it. A cannonball from the *Sky Serpent* had left a fairly large hole in the side of the ship.

When the rope reached the end of its path, the momentum of the swing pulled it back toward the engine room. Dalia repositioned her body so that she could throw the grenade with her primary hand. She did not have much time to think about any follow-up strategies.

She flipped a switch on top of the grenade as the rope neared the hole in the ship, then threw it in the direction of the engine room. The grenade struck the edge of the opening and teetered. Then the edge of the wooden plank gave way, allowing the grenade to fall inside. As the rope continued swaying, Dalia lost sight of the grenade and the engine room.

Ten seconds passed when a large explosion shook both ships. Dalia slammed against the hull of the *Sky Serpent*. The impact pushed the remainder of the air out of her lungs, but she did not let go of the rope. A single piece of wooden shrapnel flew by Dalia's head, striking the side of the ship several inches to her left. She gasped for air.

When she'd caught her breath, the enemy ship was already breaking in two, plunging downward and dragging its wooden planks to the open air below. Enemy pirates screamed as they abandoned ship.

A sudden jerk from above startled Dalia, and she looked up. Her crew was pulling the rope while Roderick instructed them to work faster.

When her feet connected with the ship's deck, her heart finally settled in her chest. She looked at Roderick, who stood several feet away, holding his shoulder as the blood continued to flow out of it. Sofia ran up to him with a piece of cloth and started applying pressure to his arm.

"Captain, come over here!" one of the pirates yelled. "We've captured the enemy captain!"

The enemy captain was flanked by two of Dalia's crewmembers, hands tied together in a bowline knot, looking at Dalia with disgust.

"You call yourself a captain, Dalia Swiftblade?" the captain muttered as he spat on the wooden floorboard in front of Dalia's feet. "You are nothing more than a traitor to the crown. I know who you are and what you are. You are—"

Dalia swiftly pulled her long blade from its sheath and pushed it through the captain's heart, extinguishing his life before he could take another breath.

****

Only twelve hours had passed since the battle. The blood spilled and lives lost lingered in the air as Dalia strolled down the side of her ship.

She planted her feet in front of Roderick, who was seated by himself, watching and admiring the workings of her crew.

"Hey!" Roderick said in a welcoming tone.

He waited for her to speak. Dalia looked like she had aged ten years since the battle, but despite that, she stood there in front of him, pretending like it hadn't even fazed her.

"Are you doing all right?" Roderick asked.

No answer came from Dalia. Instead, she asked Roderick the same question in a different form. "How's your shoulder? You think you'll make it, or do we need to cut it off?" She planted a smile on her face.

Roderick laughed. "I've been better, but I'll be all right. No need to amputate any limbs yet."

"Oh, you'll be all right," she muttered. "It's only a scratch. It will heal by the time we get to the capital."

Dalia looked down at the ground as words came out of her mouth. "I . . . I also wanted to thank you for saving my life."

Roderick blushed. "Don't mention it. I bet you would have done the same thing for me."

Dalia looked at him blankly but did not respond in kind. Instead, she changed the subject abruptly. "On a different note, where do we go next?"

"To the Castle of Madness," Roderick said.

"Castle of Madness . . . I love it. This trip is getting better and better each day," Dalia responded. "That should take us several days, so rest and let that shoulder heal. We must make a quick stop to fix up damages caused to the ship before we embark to the castle. I think you guys are going to love it there," Dalia said as she clumsily spun around and walked toward the stern, leaving Roderick to himself.

Roderick went down to the belly of the ship and knocked on Sofia's door.

"Come in," came from inside the cabin.

Roderick opened the door and walked in, finding Sofia lying curled up in bed, facing away from the door, hiding her face from onlookers. The cabin was so tiny that she could barely fully stretch out in it.

"How are you doing?" Roderick asked, standing by the bed.

"I'm doing horrible," Sofia said, staring at the wall. "I think I need some time to process everything. So many things have happened lately. So much death and destruction follows me around."

“You are not responsible for any of those deaths,” Roderick replied.

“How can you say that with a straight face?” Sofia turned around to face Roderick. “All of this is about obtaining the relics left behind for me. Directly or indirectly, it’s still my fault.”

Roderick said nothing for a long moment. When he finally spoke, his words were slow, and his eyes were dark and serious. “When I was eight, I witnessed the royal guard corralling a merchant family in a small town where I grew up. Inside their wagon, on a small piece of red fabric, the guards had found a symbol of the old kingdom. A dragon with its tail encircling wheat, symbolizing fertility; fish, symbolizing freedom; frog, symbolizing wealth; and an ant, symbolizing the unity of its people.” Roderick took a deep breath.

“The family was sentenced to death for treason. The old merchant, his young wife, and their three children begged for their lives. But it didn’t matter.

“The guards doused the wagon with a flammable liquid and torched it. I can still hear the family screaming. I can still see them perishing before my eyes.

“This is why I’m here. To restore the order and to avenge those that perished at any cost.” Roderick lowered his head, staring at the wooden floor. “If this is not enough to convince you that all of this is worth the sacrifice, I don’t know what is.”

Sofia held her breath as she stared at Roderick’s trembling lips. She gently touched his shoulder, and he flinched. “Thank you for sharing this with me. It takes courage to open up like this to a stranger. I can’t imagine witnessing all of that firsthand.”

“All I wanted to say,” Roderick continued, turning his head away from Sofia to hide persistent tears, “is that any death is better than the current situation. If nothing gets done, more people will perish from famine, unjust prosecution, slavery. You are the best thing to happen to the kingdom since Prima's takeover. At least now we have something to hope for. Hope for a better tomorrow."

"I admire your resolve," Sofia said, her eyes catching Roderick's. "And thank you for everything."

Roderick smiled. "You need to rest now. I'll need you to be ready and focused once we get to the Castle of Madness."

CHAPTER 11

Four days passed before the *Sky Serpent* arrived at a small island surrounded by the Acid Sea. An impressive castle situated on a large, volcanic rock towered over the island.

This island had been uninhabited for hundreds of years, partly because of its remote location and partly because there was no arable land to sustain life. Stories, passed from generation to generation, talked about the island forged by magic, which erected the island, together with its castle, from the bottom of the sea. Not a single story mentioned anyone ever building the castle on this ruthless yet beautiful piece of land.

After the *Sky Serpent* docked at the only accessible spot, a curious Sofia and still-injured Roderick set off for another trek. This one was much shorter in distance than the one on the island of Cratos. They did not bring any supplies with them other than the Knife of Life.

"At least, this time, we don't have to search for any caves," Sofia joked, brushing her hair from her face amidst the relentless wind.

Roderick smiled and nodded.

They climbed up a set of stairs carved into the mountain. The first twenty-two steps were greenish in color, evidence of acid eating through the concrete. It was clear that the stairs had been recently submerged during high tides. A glance upward made Sofia frown. There were three hundred steps to climb until they reached the castle's entrance.

Taking their time, they arrived at the top of the rock in twenty minutes. The castle walls were built with white marble that looked new, with no signs of wear or tear. The only way to enter the castle was through the main gate. The other option was to try to climb the slick marble walls up to one of the towers and enter the castle via small guard windows etched in its walls.

"I heard horrible stories about this place," Roderick said as they reached the top of the steps. "My father used to tell me how no one who entered this place ever returned home. The stories were told by those who brought them to the island. They talked about people jumping from the tower to their deaths. He talked about stories of people going mad, insane, of screams coming from the castle. Thinking about it gives me shivers," Roderick said.

Sofia listened intently, soaking in every single word.

As she extended her arm to try the knob, Roderick spoke up. "Are you sure about this? This could be a trap."

Sofia knew he was right, but there was nothing else she could do. If she wanted to complete her mission, this needed to be done at any cost. "I am sure."

Sofia pushed the large front door, expecting resistance, but found none.

As they entered the vast space of a grand hall, they were greeted by an unwelcome scene of hundreds of mirrors. The mirrors showed reflections of Sofia but did not show reflections of Roderick. In each of the mirrors, the reflection did not match

Sofia's actions in real life. One mirror showed her grabbing her head with both hands while screaming wildly. Another displayed Sofia punching herself in the face. Yet another mirror showed Sofia banging her head against the mirror. The reflections acted as if they were possessed. They screamed, screeched, and howled. The sounds resonated through the high ceiling of the castle, raising hairs on Sofia's arms.

When Sofia came into view of another mirror, her reflection taunted her to enter. She approached the mirror to get a better look. The reflection smiled and then lunged at her. The mirror shook but the reflection stayed contained within.

"What do you think we should do?" Roderick asked. "There must be hundreds of mirrors in here, and only one holds the secret. How do you choose the right mirror?"

"Edgar said to find my true self," Sofia said. "Does that mean that one reflection is the perfect representation of me?"

"They all look like you, but none of them act the way you do," Roderick said, scratching his head.

Sofia took a deep breath, trying to concentrate. She scanned the mirrors around her as all of her reflections seemed to wish to jump out of the mirrors and tear her apart.

Sofia sunk deep into her mind, looking for a calming sensation to guide her through this obstacle. What she found was a memory, one she had tried to suppress since finding herself in *this* dream.

Sofia's mind traveled back to her room on Willow Drive. She was standing in her bathroom, facing a reflection of someone who bore her face but was not her. It was the demon who had come into her life on the day she found out her father was not coming back. The demon who followed her wherever she went. Sometimes, he would stay hidden in the shadows, strolling casually behind her. Sometimes, he hung out inside her head. Sometimes, he presented himself in the mirror as her reflection. He was the worst kind of demon because he had her face and she could not escape him. It did not matter how hard she tried. He was always there at the worst possible time.

During that time, her mother had tried forcing Sofia to take pills, see a psychiatrist, or rediscover herself. This was all in hopes of reclaiming her daughter.

Sofia wanted badly to kill her demon. She wanted to see pain in her demon's eyes, the way she was feeling the pain of losing her father, but he would always reappear stronger and more ruthless than ever before.

Sofia came back to her senses as she stood in the middle of the mirror hall. She surveyed the room, making a connection between her memory and her current situation. *This is still my dream . . . unless my demon is trying to play mind games with me. It wouldn't be the first time. I guess there is only one way to find out.*

Sofia pulled the Knife of Life from her tunic. She unwrapped it from a piece of cloth that protected it, lifted the blade in front of her face, and looked at it with admiration. She smiled, full of confidence and rage at the same time. *Follow your instinct.* Sofia raised the knife and looked over at Roderick.

"Edgar said destroying the wrong mirror would mean certain death." Roderick nodded. "Then what I'm about to do should be fine," Sofia said, slashing the closest mirror bearing her reflection.

The reflection in the mirror stumbled back, its muscles stiffening. Moments later, the reflection lurched forward, screaming.

Roderick pulled his blade out.

Sofia turned in his direction. “Let me deal with this alone,” Sofia said. “I have some unfinished business I need to deal with.”

Roderick stepped aside, still holding on to his weapon.

Sofia moved to another mirror, placed the edge of the knife up against it, and slashed, leaving a small cut on the surface. Her reflection in the mirror tried jumping out, its hands stretched toward Sofia’s neck, but was stopped short by the glass. Sofia felt good about it. She knew her demon was hiding behind one of the reflections.

She readied herself and then leaped into a cutting spree. She ran from one mirror to another, slashing them one by one, leaving angry reflections in its wake. She wanted the reflections to feel pain as much as she felt it. She wanted to be free of her demon.

She ran through the hall of mirrors, slashing each mirror quickly and efficiently. They kept coming, and she kept slashing. This sudden infusion of rage helped Sofia cut through at least two hundred mirrors with the same end result—making the reflections angrier and thirstier for blood.

Sofia sliced another mirror, and another, and another. The last mirror that she slashed sent an odd sensation through her left bicep, like a paper cut. She stopped and looked at her tunic. The left sleeve showed a cut in the fabric. As she pushed the sleeve up, Sofia observed blood sliding down her arm. The cut was not deep, but it stung.

Sofia tried to get a sense of how she had cut herself, ignoring the screams coming from the mirror in front of her. She was so accustomed to hearing them that she was oblivious to the reflection.

Sofia lifted her head and looked at herself in the mirror. Her reflection tried to jump out at her but was short of succeeding. A shocking sensation overtook Sofia as the reflection of herself bled from her left bicep, just as she was. *My God, it worked.*

She swiftly moved to the previous mirror. Sofia's reflection did not bleed at all. Still in disbelief, Sofia returned to the last mirror and made another small incision on the reflection's left thigh. Instantaneous pain hit her left thigh.

The reflection flashed its demon teeth at her—skinny, long, and pointy. The reflection's eyes turned into the eyes of the wolf that her father had killed to save her when she was a little girl. She would always remember those evil eyes . . . Eyes of a killer.

There was no more doubt in Sofia's mind. She raised her hand that was clutching the Knife of Life, handle facing the mirror, and, with one swift, precise strike, she brought the knife down on the mirror.

Cobwebs and cracks riddled the mirror as the reflection inside screamed bloody murder before it slowly dissipated from view. The glass shattered onto the marble floor. The screams stopped.

"I finally killed my demon," Sofia said to herself. A burden seemed to lift from her shoulders.

She looked at the broken mirror with more attention, realizing that there was an opening in the wall behind it that contained a medium-sized wooden box with the same animal symbols as the Knife of Life and her bracelet.

She pulled out the box and carefully opened it on the floor. The box contained a stack of tan, blank papers. Nothing more. *The magic paper.*

She closed the wooden box, leaving the paper inside untouched, and walked past one of the mirrors. To her surprise, the reflection in the mirror looked like her, mimicking her exact movements, facial expressions, and the wooden box that she carried.

Sofia turned around and walked over to Roderick, who stood cemented to the floor in the middle of the large hall.

"Are you okay?" Roderick asked, looking at Sofia's new injuries. "You are bleeding!"

Sofia smiled as she lifted the box. "It's okay. It's only a paper cut." She opened the box, revealing what was inside.

"You got it!" Roderick exclaimed happily.

"I can't believe you doubted me."

"Never," Roderick said as they rushed out of the castle and descended the stairs toward the *Sky Serpent.*

CHAPTER 12

Sofia sat in the middle of Dalia's wounded ship, holding the Knife of Life and the box of magic paper in her hands. She did not need anyone to tell her how much she had accomplished in the short time that she had spent in Thalia.

As usual, over the past several days, Roderick came to join her. "I have no words to describe how impressed I am," Roderick announced as he sat next to her.

"Thank you," Sofia said, blushing. "This was something I had to do on my own and I didn't want to drag someone else down with me in case I made a mistake. It wouldn't be the first time I made a mistake in my life. I am no stranger to bad luck." Sofia closed the lid on the box and switched her gaze toward the deep blue skies surrounding the *Sky Serpent*.

"I learned something about myself yesterday," she confessed. "I learned that despite the demons we keep inside of us, we should never give up. They might seem stronger than us or even smarter, but if you stop fighting, you don't stand a chance of ever reclaiming your life. We can win against all odds if we put our will to it."

Sofia took a deep breath.

“I will tell you one thing,” she continued. “I wanted to say this many times before, but I know it’s not going to be enough.”

“What’s that?” Roderick asked.

“I wanted to—and I needed to—say thank you for everything you have done for me so far. I know I doubted you more than once. As a matter of fact, I doubted and still doubt all of this.”

Roderick’s face turned deep red. “You don’t know how much this means to me. But I don’t do what I do for a thank you. I do it for other reasons.”

Sofia smiled. “I know you do, and that’s why a simple thank you doesn’t do it justice.”

****

The following day, Sofia woke up from a deep sleep when one of Dalia’s trustworthy lookouts yelled, “Land! Land up ahead!”

She picked up a hairbrush Dalia had given her before they had landed on the island of Cratos. She ran it through her straight hair, enough to separate some of the tangles.

Above her, the wooden planks screeched steadily. Dalia was having a parental conversation with her crew. This happened each time they were about to enter or leave a harbor. Dalia’s crew knew their jobs, but it was painful to watch them run around, clueless, without proper direction from their captain. At times, they were useless, like a gang of annoying kids bugging their parents to buy them ice cream or chocolate.

Moments later, Sofia recognized the sound of the anchors being released from the ship, followed by the tying off of ropes, which eventually led to the shutting down of the ship’s engines.

They had finally arrived at their final destination—the floating islands of Atmosfera.

Once she finished brushing her hair, Sofia tied her blonde locks tightly into a ponytail. She washed her face with water from a ceramic vase next to the nightstand, then softly ran a cotton towel over her face, drying it with extreme care.

She emerged from the lower deck of the ship refreshed, ready for the next adventure.

Roderick was already there, preparing his satchel. "Good morning," he spoke, loud enough so his words could reach Sofia.

"Good morning to you, too! Did you sleep well?" Sofia's positive attitude radiated through her joyful response.

"I slept fine," Roderick said, but did not elaborate. "I've got stuff ready to go. I don't think I have any space left in the satchel."

When Sofia looked overboard, she was greeted by an impressive sight. The *Sky Serpent* found itself surrounded by the floating islands of Atmosfera. There were a dozen or so visible from the ship. They were all of different sizes and shapes, floating in the air like birthday balloons. Some of them were covered in grassy meadows, some in rugged mountainous terrain, some fully engulfed with trees. Sofia could not decide which one she liked best.

She welcomed the strange new scenery. All of it brought her back to memories of her parents' camping and trekking. However, Sofia's favorite spot had always been close to home. Near the lake not far from her house, there was a large stump, the remnants of a red spruce.

The stump resembled a throne. Sofia would often sit on it, pretending to be the queen of her kingdom, the woods, relinquished to her without a fight. She would stare at the glossy blue lake, considering all the requests and demands of her people, the critters, and the birds.

"There are so many of them," Sofia gasped when Dalia walked up behind her, disrupting her piece of serenity.

"This once was the most beautiful of all the places in the Thalian kingdom," Dalia offered.

"Once was?" Sofia asked.

"You heard right, little princess," Dalia said as she moved to the left of Sofia.

"The queen exploited these islands and enslaved all of their inhabitants. She drained all their resources and, once a year, she sent ships to collect the bounty. People worked the entire year tirelessly and had nothing to show for it. Many of them starved to death. The queen would often punish entire families or sometimes entire towns if one person did not meet the quota she randomly came up with."

Sofia kept finding herself surprised by every new detail regarding the kingdom—her kingdom—and each time, the details were more gruesome and troubling. This was the first time since the beginning of this dream that Sofia wished she was in charge so she could make changes for the better. She was tired of hearing these horror stories of the queen and her despicable rule.

Sofia looked below the ship. The floating island where the *Sky Serpent* was anchored looked nothing like the others surrounding it. This particular island was covered with stone rubble of what used to be the City of Bones. There was nothing there now. It smelled and looked like death and suffering. Clear evidence of Queen Prima's ruthless rule over the kingdom and a reminder for everyone who tried to defy her rule and authority.

Roderick, Sofia, and two of Dalia's trusted crew landed on the city's remnants below. There was something eerie about standing in a place that had once flourished with life but now stood lifeless.

Sofia glanced over the skyline of the rubble city that was nothing but a concrete jungle with hints of greenery protruding from within. It reminded Sofia of the TV show she used to watch with her dad, *The Walking Dead.* The City of Bones resembled the post-apocalyptic city of Atlanta. All she needed now were zombies to pop up behind the rubble.

Roderick took the lead, walking toward the center of the city, paying attention to every nook and cranny. "Tell me if you see something of interest," Roderick told Sofia as he continued his stroll forward.

Sofia understood that Roderick's faith in her decision-making had increased tenfold since the island of Cratos. She felt pressured to continue her streak of good luck in finding the right solutions to the puzzles left behind by the Grand Witch.

Sofia's confidence grew with each step. She needed to find the blueprint, and then her job was half-done, as long as defeating the queen did not complicate things beyond what she expected. It was one thing to think positively about the resolution to her current situation but an entirely different thing to achieve it.

It wasn't until they came closer to the taller buildings that Sofia noticed that the structures were constructed from bones and clearly not human ones.

"My God," Sofia gasped. "Are those bones?"

Roderick looked at her as he touched the bony wall of a half-ruined building. "I think the name of the island might have given you a hint," Roderick said, offering a smile. Blushing, he cleared his throat. "Well, these bones are from ancient creatures that lived here centuries ago when the floating islands of Atmosfera were one big floating island. I learned from Master Fry that the island separated into many smaller islands during the second solar storm. All the creatures on the island died during the cataclysm. When humans populated the islands, they used the bones to construct these impressive buildings."

"These creatures had to be enormous," Sofia said, admiring the sight before her. "Way bigger than the dinosaurs."

"Dino—what?" Roderick inquired.

Sofia remembered that she had never told Roderick about dinosaurs when she had given him a lesson about the world that she had come from—or a dream that he thought she had created.

"Never mind," Sofia said as she touched the bony wall that Roderick had touched moments earlier. The wall was white, like it had been bleached, and as smooth as satin. Sofia imagined these ancient creatures roaming the island before they all disappeared at the snap of a finger, like her childhood.

Their progress was slow as they trekked over the rubble that stood in their path, unwilling to offer a clear path to wherever they were heading. The sun shone, casting its rays on the white, bony structures of the City of Bones, making the surface hot to the touch.

Sofia and Roderick looked around, searching for a clue, but other than the sea of white structures, there was nothing else that caught their interest.

Where did she hide the blueprint? Sofia asked herself. *It could be under any of these bones. There must be something else around here. She had to have left a clue.*

As they continued traveling through the rubble city, Roderick's attention kept shifting from one building to another, surveying the area for any potential dangers. He took his job seriously and did not want to put Sofia in any unnecessary danger if he could prevent it.

His eyes kept returning to one particular building. It looked the same as the one before it and the one after it. And yet, he found himself flinching

"Is everything okay?" Sofia asked.

"I . . . I don't know," Roderick answered, still keeping his gaze upward. "I have the feeling someone is watching us from above. I need you to stand close to me. I have a weird feeling about this."

The trek turned into a hike that eventually led to a pure rock climb. They navigated the ruins under Roderick's lead, interrupted every five hundred feet so that he could reassess the threat level.

As the four hikers conquered yet another mountain of rubble, they found themselves in what was once the main square. The remnants of a fountain protruding from the center of the rubble were the only evidence left of its former glory.

Roderick stopped in his tracks and focused on something in a building to their immediate right. He stared intently at a branch jutting out from a window on the third floor, now more like a ground floor because the rubble reached up to it.

"I need you to stay here and not move," Roderick declared as he pulled a blade from his waist and moved toward the window. The little branch had moved next to it, yet there was no wind.

Roderick approached the window and, with a series of small steps, stepped inside the ruined structure. He navigated through several rooms, all littered with chunks of ceiling or other debris.

He moved silently, like a predator approaching its prey. He navigated another corner, then walked through two more rooms before a sound caught his attention.

A shadow appeared in a room adjacent to the one he found himself in. The shadow moved and became more obvious as the person moved toward the window overlooking the square. Roderick raised his blade as he moved to the doorframe. He peeked inside, only to find a boy of twelve or thirteen years old.

The boy wore a gray jumpsuit and had dreads with small blades resembling arrowheads attached to the ends of each. He watched the square attentively, tilting his head to the side.

Roderick took several steps into the room. But as he moved closer, he stepped on a small rock, making enough noise to gain the boy's attention.

When the boy spun around, Roderick was already before him, his blade flush against the boy's neck. The boy's eyes widened. He had the face of a defeated man.

"Not a word or I'll slice you before you open your mouth," Roderick warned. Then he instructed the boy to slowly turn away from him as he moved behind his back. The blade of Roderick's sword never moved from the boy's throat.

They moved lethargically toward the window through which Roderick entered the building. Excited to proclaim his small victory to Sofia and the others, Roderick yelled, "Look what I found!"

When no one responded to his excitement, Roderick peeked around the boy's head, facing the ruined square. His jaw dropped. Eight boys, dressed and built like the one he held hostage, circled Sofia and Dalia's men.

These boy soldiers swung their hair in circles like a lasso. Some of them had small darts attached to their dreads, while others had a single blade attached to ponytails formed of many small dreads. There was one boy who had small balls with spikes sticking out of them.

"I suggest you let him go," someone announced from a nearby building.

Roderick searched for the person who had spoken. Moments later, the source presented himself. A teenage boy about Roderick's age exited the building directly across from Roderick. Half of his face was covered with thallium, while the other half was human flesh. He wore a red tunic, high collars peppered with gold skull accents, over a pair of black pants tucked into a pair of matching boots. A tattoo of a skull was visible on his forearm. The boy jumped from the second floor and landed smoothly on his feet, like a cat.

The other boys slightly bowed their heads in his presence.

"It looks like we have a stalemate. I say you let us go, then I will release your soldier," Roderick demanded.

The half-masked boy laughed wholeheartedly. "You call this a stalemate? Let me introduce myself first," he said, smiling widely. "My name is Hazard, and this is my city. You trespass, take my soldier hostage, and then make demands? I should remind you that by the time you cut the boy's throat, your three friends will lie dead. Your death will quickly follow theirs. We might lose one of ours, but all four of you will perish."

Roderick was sweating profusely.

Roderick walked his hostage down to the center of the square until he entered the circle of long-haired soldiers. He planted his feet next to Sofia. “All right,” he said. “I will now release your soldier and will put my weapon down. Can I have your promise not to act before we have time to explain ourselves?”

Hazard looked at him and then looked at his soldiers. “You have my word.”

Roderick released the boy soldier from his grip, and the boy moved away, reuniting with his fellow soldiers. Once he entered the circle of his peers, the boy soldier swung his long hair around as he took a fight-ready posture.

Roderick placed his sword on the ground in front of him and signaled to Dalia’s men to do the same. He did not count on the fact that pirates lived by the rule of no surrender.

Dalia’s men exchanged looks before they launched a surprise attack. However, the offensive was over before it had even begun. Both pirates were cut down by the array of weaponized hair flying through the air. They fell to the rocky ground as the weapons returned to the hands of boy soldiers.

“Wait!” Roderick yelled. “Please, don’t. They were not with us.”

Hazard raised his arm to signal to the others to seize the attack. “You are trying to tell me that these men, that you walked with and stood with, are not with you? I would love to hear your explanation. Please, amuse me,” Hazard said, keeping his arm in the air.

“I promised to explain everything, and I will, but I can’t do it if I’m dead.”

Hazard smiled. “Looks like some common sense has finally kicked in,” he said. He moved closer to Roderick until he stood several feet away. "You said you have some explaining to do. I can't wait to hear all about it, especially the part about how these two were not with you."

Everyone laughed except for Roderick and Sofia. Sofia stood, frightened, but did not intervene.

Hazard continued, "As far as I know, tax day was several weeks ago, and we don't harbor any fugitives, so what would the queen possibly want from us?"

Roderick looked at Hazard, thanking the gods for giving him a way out. "We are not here for either of those reasons. We are not here on behalf of the crown."

"Interesting," Hazard said. "So, you are here to loot? I have to disappoint you. There is nothing to loot around here. Look around."

"Let me explain these two men first," Roderick said. "These men belong to a ship captain by the name of Dalia Swiftblade. We hired her to bring us here."

"Bring you to the City of Bones?" Hazard asked.

"Not quite," Roderick answered. "The two of us," Roderick continued, pointing at Sofia, "are on a mission to find answers about . . ." Roderick stopped for a moment.

Before he could say more, Sofia jumped in. "We are on a mission to bring the light magic back to life so that we can bring down the queen."

Hazard turned his head toward Sofia, then back toward Roderick. "You two are on a mission to bring down the queen?" He could barely finish the sentence before he burst into laughter. The rest of his soldiers joined in. "Oh my, I have not laughed like this in a long time," Hazard said. "Let me tell you something. There is no defeating the queen. The only person who could have done that is Princess Elan, who, by the way, is as dead as one can be."

Sofia smiled widely, catching Hazard by surprise. "What if I tell you that miracles do happen?"

Hazard examined Sofia's face. His eyebrows formed a single line, but he did not offer any input.

Sofia pulled up the sleeve of her tunic, revealing the Bracelet of Life etched into her skin.

Hazard stood motionless for a moment, and then he moved closer to Sofia, not losing sight of the bracelet. He reached out as far as his arm could go until his fingers touched Sofia's bracelet. Then Hazard dropped to his knees. "Your Highness," he said, placing his forehead onto Sofia's palm. "This is indeed a miracle," he spoke with his head bowed. "We prayed for this day to come, but our hopes were lost after word got out that you were dead."

Sofia took Hazard by the arm and helped him up. This moment eased the tension, and the other boy soldiers released their hair weapons.

"I am the leader of the Order of the Skull, sworn protectors of the old crown," Hazard said.

Sofia followed her intuition as she pulled the Knife of Life and a stack of magic papers from her tunic.

As if confronted by some invisible power, Hazard and his crew could not stop staring at the ancient artifacts they had only heard about in stories.

"We came to the City of Bones to find the blueprint to bring light magic to life," Sofia said. "Can you help us locate it?"

Hazard smiled. "I will not help you locate it. I'll take you straight to it!"

Roderick and Sofia exchanged grins.

CHAPTER 13

Hazard led Roderick and Sofia through a maze of rubble streets, toppled buildings, and underground passages until they arrived in front of a wooden door deep beneath the city. Upon entry, Sofia and Roderick found themselves surrounded by a dozen long-haired soldiers. There was an equal number of boys and girls in the group.

The large area stretched into several smaller rooms. Naphtha lamps burned throughout the area, as sunshine was forbidden from ever entering this secret underground hideaway.

Roderick and Sofia continued to follow Hazard through a series of corridors under the constant scrutiny of the wandering eyes of young boys and girls. After several turns, they reached a dead end and stood before another wooden door as unimpressive as the one they had used to enter the hideaway spot below the City of Rubble.

Hazard used a key that hung on a chain around his neck to unlock the door. The door swung inward, and they entered the room.

Hazard walked up to an old wooden desk that was sitting in the middle of the room. He pulled out a key from the only drawer in it. The key looked identical to the one that he had used to unlock the door. He approached another piece of furniture that looked like an armoire. This piece sat up against the wall opposite the entry door.

Hazard opened the wooden door, revealing some old clothes and boxes. He shifted several boxes around, then removed one heavy wooden box and placed it on the floor next to him. The space on the shelf revealed a small hole in the armoire. Hazard inserted the key from the desk into the hole and turned it twice counterclockwise, producing a clicking sound with each turn. Then Hazard opened a small, wooden door in the back of the armoire and pulled out a thin thallium box from it. Sofia did not need an explanation of what it was because of the unique baby blue glow it produced.

Hazard removed the box and placed it on the table in the center of the room. The box was two inches thick, eight inches high, and five inches wide. There was a small hole on the side that looked like another keyhole.

Hazard met Sofia's eyes as he spoke. "Can I please have the Knife of Life, Princess?"

Sofia handed over the knife without thinking twice about it.

Hazard admired the knife for a moment. "It is remarkable. I never thought I would see it in person." He fiddled with the knife for another moment or two, then placed the tip into a keyhole on the side of the box. It fit perfectly.

"Princess, you need to open the box because it will not allow anyone other than the bearer of the Bracelet of Life to do so."

Sofia reached down and grabbed hold of the knife with her right hand. Hesitating slightly, she turned the knife key once counterclockwise. The sound of the knife turning produced a clicking sound, and then the top of the box opened, revealing a single piece of paper in its belly.

Sofia and Roderick moved closer to inspect the box's contents.

"Is this what I think it is?" Sofia asked.

Hazard nodded. "It's the blueprint for creating light magic."

"This is it," Sofia proclaimed. "The final piece of the puzzle."

Relief and happiness swept over Sofia as she unfolded the piece of paper from the box. It revealed the blueprint for creating the seven creatures from her bracelet. Each picture was accompanied by several smaller diagrams showing specific folds and cuts on how to create the paper animals. The paper was bluish, and the prints stood out from the background. There was no doubt which animal was which, even though there were no names listed on the paper. The precision of the prints was impressive.

Sofia stared at the paper in her hand and remembered Edgar's lesson on how to create magic. She knew creating magic was not going to be a cakewalk, but she had gotten this far and had to try.

Excitement struck Sofia's mind, washing away all other thoughts. She took a piece of magic paper from her satchel and stretched it onto the table in front of her. She picked up the Knife of Life and looked at it for a second. It looked as if the knife had slightly changed its appearance. It was more beautiful, and the baby blue glow radiating from the blade was more intense.

Sofia looked over at the blueprint and then back at the paper in front of her. Her body was under a lot of pressure to do the right thing. She followed the instructions on the blueprint on how to assemble a paper mouse. She folded the paper carefully, trying to match the lines on the blueprint. Several times, she had to readjust the folds because they did not line up perfectly. When she was done folding the paper, she sighed deeply.

"I think I'm done," Sofia declared with a sense of relief.

Sofia took the Knife of Life and cut the excess paper from the folds. Words from Edgar came into her head. *Remember, one mistake while cutting the magic paper will dissipate the paper into nothingness. You must cut it precisely by the lines of the fold.*

Sofia did not need more pressure than she was already under, so she pushed the thought out of her head and took the knife in her right hand. She placed the tip of the blade on one end of the folded paper. With her hand still shaking, Sofia moved the knife's blade over the paper folds. *Keep steady.*

After more than twenty seconds of moving the blade over the paper, she stopped breathing to steady herself. As she took a deep breath to bring some air into her lungs, one jerking motion of her hand pushed the knife off the fold, slicing a small portion of the paper origami. In an instant, the paper fold disintegrated before her eyes into nothingness.

"Oh no!" she gasped as her eyes met Roderick's.

"It's okay," he replied. "You are under a lot of stress. It would help if you can find peace within yourself to calm down. There is enough paper left to assemble many more of these. Find your inner peace and try again."

"Easier said than done," Sofia replied. "I didn't think cutting paper would cause more stress than facing execution by a circular saw."

Sofia excused herself from the safety of the underground lair, leaving two worried faces behind. She walked and climbed layers of rubble until she stood on top of a building overlooking two floating islands in the distance. There was a solitary tree sitting on top of a ruined building dotted with beautiful rosy flowers and birds of different kinds.

She tried clearing her head of all poison and garbage that had accumulated over the past two weeks. *No, for the past two years . . ..* The problem was that this was easier said than done. Sofia still carried the weight of her father's disappearance with her.

She sat below the tree on the hill, staring at the horizon, reflecting on her accomplishments and upcoming dangers. *This tree is lucky. It has the best view of the island beyond the City of Bones.*

The other side of the island was the complete opposite of the rubble city. Green, lush fields covered with yellow and red flower tops. The background was a blue canvas of several shades, featuring a yellow dot shining on top of it. *It's beautiful.* There was something uplifting and calming about this place, despite what lay beyond it.

Her head was still a mishmash of different emotions that she wanted to sort out once and for all. She could not find the words to describe her mental state at the moment. Her head was empty one second and full the other. She desperately wanted all that was negative out of her head, out and gone forever, never to return.

She thought about the Castle of Madness and how she had felt when she had broken the mirror. She had felt relief as pounds and pounds of invisible weight had left her body in an instant. She wanted to feel that way all the time and find the key to her happiness again. She only wished she knew where she'd left the key. *I hope I can still find it.*

Her life had changed drastically. For the first time since she had found herself in this new land, she did not care whether or not this was all real. She was real. She was needed. People cared about her. She had a purpose in life. Sofia now wished that her mother did not spend all that time, effort, and money on trying to help her find what she had found here.

With eyes beginning to cloud with tears, she glanced over the horizon stretching before her, looking for a hint of inspiration. She thought about magic, her parents, Roderick.

She was surprised to find Roderick in her thoughts, but he was now a part of her life. So too was Dalia, the infamous girl in black, her friend.

Sofia pulled out the Knife of Life from her pocket, followed by a piece of magic paper and the blueprint. She looked at the blueprint once more, staring at the diagram of a butterfly. Sofia flipped, folded, and shifted the piece of paper in her hands. With the last fold, Sofia brought the knife to its creases and followed the lines carefully.

As the knife crisscrossed from fold to fold, excess paper hung down by a sliver. It was one last touch of the blade that separated the excess paper from the butterfly origami.

Sofia held the paper butterfly in her right palm, eyes closed. Out of nowhere, wind appeared, caressing her face and arms, tipping the paper butterfly from her palm, and pushing it into the air.

Some invisible power lifted Sofia up as she transformed into something otherworldly, something beautiful. She opened her eyes and stared at the tree with pink flowers in front of her. The flowers smelled sweet, almost the same as the lilies behind her house in Maine.

She turned around in the air and stared at a giant standing in front of her. She flinched and retreated. When she found the courage to face the threat before her, her own motionless body stood there. The Bracelet of Life subtly glowed on her wrist. Sofia was witnessing magic.

Her butterfly body danced around the sole tree on the hill. She landed on one of the pink flowers decorating the tree and smelled it. *Beautiful. I never imagined magic would smell so beautiful.*

Sofia felt as if she had accomplished something important in her life that many other people would not get a chance to experience. Sofia smiled as her confidence grew. She gave herself a mental pat on the back. *I created magic.*

****

A short distance away, in the shadows of the rubble, a set of eyes watched Sofia. Then the sound of typing into a small handheld device overtook the sound of the person's breathing. The last keystroke sent the message.

All sources acquired. Mission accomplished.

CHAPTER 14

When Sofia returned to the safety of the underground safe house, Roderick and Hazard sat on a couch with their legs crossed at their ankles, waiting to hear the news.

"Did you do it?" Roderick asked as he jumped up on his feet.

She looked at him as she pulled a box out of her tunic, revealing a paper origami of a butterfly. "I created one," Sofia said.

"And?" Roderick asked.

"And then this happened," Sofia answered as she released the paper origami from her right palm into the air, showing off her new ability.

Everyone in the safe house looked on, stunned, as Sofia flew above their heads in the form of a beautiful orange butterfly with black dots and stripes crisscrossing her wings.

"It's beautiful, and it's true," Hazard said as he dropped to his knees.

All the boys and girls followed Hazard's lead.

Roderick grinned as Sofia flew above him. After several minutes of worship, the little butterfly landed in Sofia's right palm, transforming itself back into its paper form and bringing Sofia's human body back to life.

****

On their way to Dalia's ship, Hazard and his men carried the two dead pirates while Roderick and Sofia walked beside them. As they stood below the *Sky Serpent*, Dalia and her men lined up along the ship's main deck, aiming their weapons at the group below.

"It's all right! They are friends!" Sofia yelled. "Dalia, we need you to come down so we can have a word in private!"

"They don't look like friends to me!" Dalia yelled from the ship. "Friends don't bring dead men as a homecoming gift!"

"It's not what it looks like," Roderick offered. "It's complicated, but they mean no harm."

Dalia crossed her arms, looking down at Roderick and the others. "You better have a good explanation, or we're going to have a problem."

Dalia and several of her men met Sofia, Roderick, Hazard, and his soldiers on the ground below her floating ship. Sofia explained to Dalia why her men had been killed, but even after having a reasonably good explanation, Dalia accepted the bodies but did not agree with the assessment of why they had to die.

As Dalia's and Hazard's men worked on the body transfer, Hazard sheepishly approached Sofia. "Princess, please allow me to join you on your mission to the capital. This is what we trained for since we were selected for this sacred duty."

Sofia considered Hazard's proposal for a moment but shook her head in the end. "I'm sorry, Hazard. I thank all of you for what you have done, for believing in me. I plan to accomplish this on my own and don't want to drag anyone else into my own problems. I've already lost people I care about. I don't want to add to the list. I thank you from the bottom of my heart, but consider yourselves relieved of your duty . . . at least for now. You protected the blueprint for all these years, and for me, that's more than enough." Sofia extended her arm toward Hazard, expecting to shake his hand. Instead, he kneeled in front of her and kissed her hand.

Hazard then stood up, looked Sofia in the eyes, and yelled, "For the princess, for the crown, for Thalia!"

All other boy and girl soldiers yelled in unison as Sofia and Roderick boarded the *Sky Serpent.*

As the ship started to gain altitude, Hazard and his long-haired soldiers retreated behind a series of tall, half-destroyed buildings. They climbed the ruins of the City of Bones with such ease as if they had been born of it and now it was their playground. And it was—the only one they had ever had.

The trip back to the capital would take a whole week of flying. This would be the time to

plan what to do next. Sofia knew it was crucial that they see Bartholomeu once they arrived in

the capital because he could direct them toward the secret passage to the queen's castle.

Over the next several days of travel, Sofia spent most of her time below the main deck, working on her paper animals. She folded and cut multiple papers, destroying two by improper cuts or folds. She eventually managed to assemble a bat, a fox, a bear, a mouse, and an eagle. She looked at the blueprint of a dragon but could not find enough courage to assemble it. There was something about dragons that Sofia had read or watched as a kid that scared her. She also knew that the dragon was the strongest of all creatures. She had to have it at her disposal before their arrival at the capital.

After many hours of inner debate, Sofia made a paper dragon and added it to the box.

****

The *Sky Serpent* safely docked at Portal City's airship harbor, flanked by three other ships that were smaller in size. The harbor was bustling with life at this time of day, which was not unusual because it was the fifth week of the rainy season. The streets were packed with merchants, hawkers, buyers, common folk, and kids running around. The chaos of the harbor stretched to the entertainment quarters, which housed a multitude of pubs and merchant stores selling everything from seafood to expensive jewelry, all made in Portal City.

"What do we do now?" Roderick asked.

"I'm kind of hungry," Sofia replied, touching her stomach.

"I wouldn't mind some hot soup to satisfy my cravings," Roderick added.

"Then I suggest you go to Central Square; they have some good pubs there. Little expensive, but worth it," Dalia said without a hint of hesitation as she threw a single gold coin toward Roderick. Then she pointed at a wanted poster glued to a nearby building. "But before you do that, I suggest you cover your faces. And, as far as this coin goes, I expect you to repay me for it once the job is done."

Roderick nodded as he placed the gold coin into his pocket.

Sofia and Roderick covered their faces with bandanas they had taken earlier from the ship. Then they separated from their entourage and veered left into the merchant district, following the sign for Central Square.

At the same time, Dalia and some of her crew continued straight to the entertainment district to douse themselves in alcohol at one of the local pubs.

The streets of Portal City looked refreshing to Sofia, almost resembling the streets of old Prague or Munich. Flower pots hung outside windows, freshly washed façades in every imaginable color, gothic-looking buildings, but above all, friendly people.

Sofia needed a good day's rest. She was anxious to explore the city, but she also craved a nice, fluffy bed where she could rest her exhausted body. She slept on Dalia's ship but, thanks to the small, uncomfortable bed, was always more tired after a long sleep.

Roderick and Sofia strolled through the streets of the old city, passing many merchant stores until they found themselves in front of a flashy jewelry store by the name of Portal City Jewelers. An impressive array of custom-made jewelry was displayed at the front window, but none of the pieces had price tags on them. This was when Sofia realized that the entire city was paperless.

The closest thing to paper was the many cloth wanted posters featuring her face.

They passed several more blocks of merchant shops, followed by some opulently decorated residential buildings. They eventually arrived at the center of the city, which featured the central square. It was squeezed between towering buildings, some up to five stories high, with a sizable fountain in the middle of the square depicting Queen Prima on a dragon, waving her sword at the heavens. This was the first time Sofia saw what Prima looked like. She approached the fountain and looked up at the statue of a girl in her twenties wearing a crown. Sofia looked at her face, searching for any resemblance between them but could not find any.

Despite the cold night, the water in the fountain was running flawlessly. A shoe shiner sat in the doorway of the shoe shops, patiently waiting for customers. Not too far from the shoe shiner, some fifty feet away to the right, stood a black carriage with golden trim and two beautiful dark stallions harnessed to the front of it. No one stood around the carriage, but the stallions kept kicking the cobblestones with their hooves.

"What do you think about that one?" Roderick said, pointing at a pub advertising the best soup in town.

"Sounds like a plan," Sofia said quickly. She did not intend to be picky about food when her stomach was growling.

They walked in the direction of the pub. Even though it was the fifth week of the rainy season, the place was nearly empty. They found an empty table near the entrance and claimed it without waiting to be seated by the host.

A middle-aged waitress gave them a look of annoyance from across the room as she moved in their direction. Her slow walk felt infinite to Sofia. When she finally arrived at their table, she pulled a wet, dirty-looking rag from her front pocket and cleaned the table with it. Then she picked up an ashtray from the middle of the table so that she could clean the portion of the table obscured by it. She did not bother to clean the contents of the ashtray itself.

As she returned the ashtray to its spot, she rudely asked, "What can I get you two?"

Roderick pressed his lips tight, then offered a smile. "What do you have to offer? Do you have a menu?"

The waitress frowned at him but offered, "Oh yes, the menu. We have a soup and we have some bread. You ready to order?"

"I guess we'll take two soups and a loaf of bread. Thank you," Roderick replied.

With their orders placed, the waitress looked at Sofia and Roderick, squaring up her shoulders. "You're not from around here, are you?"

"No," Sofia said. She shifted her gaze to meet Roderick's eyes, hoping that the waitress's curiosity would end with that question. Eventually, the waitress shook her head as she walked toward the kitchen.

Several steps into her retreat, the waitress yelled to someone in the kitchen, "Give me two soups and a loaf of bread for these two out-of-towners!"

Roderick and Sofia exchanged looks and discreetly laughed over the waitress's attitude.

Not even five minutes after their order, two bowls of soup found themselves on their table. The soup was simply delicious. It reminded Sofia of her mother's homemade chicken soup.

Roderick tore the bread in half and handed one half to Sofia. She grabbed it and dug her teeth deep into it, tearing into the bread like an animal pulling on some gamey meat.

"Do you think that eating bread like this is princess-like?" Sofia asked Roderick.

He looked at her for a brief second and then burst out laughing.

Sofia followed with even louder laughter as a small piece of unchewed bread escaped her mouth and landed on the floor in front of her.

As their stomachs sang of satisfaction, shards of glass suddenly pricked Sofia's skin. The shrill crash of the explosion seemed to come a split second later. Raising her arm to shield her face, Sofia saw the windows surrounding their table had shattered, gaping holes where the glass used to be.

Roderick and Sofia rushed for the front door. Roderick grabbed the doorknob, but it did not budge.

"The door is locked!" he yelled as they both turned around to face the kitchen. Oddly, the pub was empty of people. Even the annoying waitress had disappeared.

The pub filled with gray smoke, but there was no heat accompanying it and no fire in sight. Sofia smelled the smoke, which left a sweet taste in her mouth. *It tastes like sugar.*

Roderick grabbed Sofia by the forearm and pulled her after him, moving toward the kitchen. His legs then collapsed against his wishes, but he continued to fight gravity by lifting himself from the ground. Several labored steps further, Sofia pulled Roderick back. His body jerked, and he gasped for air as the room became fully engulfed by gray smoke.

Roderick looked toward Sofia, who lay on the floor, motionless. Then his mind began to grow cloudy.

His head spun as someone, a mere outline in the cloud of smoke, reached for Sofia's motionless body. Roderick stared at a tall man with a dark mask covering his entire face.

He tried to fight the sleepy feeling but in vain. Moments later, Roderick closed his eyes.

CHAPTER 15

Dalia made her way to Central Square to look for her passengers. When she turned the corner into the square, she spotted the broken window at the nearby pub. She approached the front door with her hand on top of her weapon.

The taste of burned sugar touched her lips.

Dalia pulled a short blade from her belt as she warily opened the door. The pub was empty. Chairs had been knocked over, and a thick layer of smoke clung to the ceiling. Dalia pulled a bandana from her pocket and tied it over her mouth and nose as she proceeded indoors.

In the kitchen, she found a cook and two waitresses on the floor, motionless but breathing steadily.

Dalia moved to an adjacent room where three more bodies lay. Dalia approached the door, stepping over one of the waitresses as she reached for the doorknob. The sweetness of whatever she tasted made her dizzy.

Dalia turned the knob. The room was dark at first, but once the door was opened fully, the light from the kitchen illuminated a pantry full of flour and oil. She moved back toward the exit, stepping over the same waitress who was now mumbling something.

On her way out, she came across a small container near the broken window with white foam surrounding its greenish metallic body.

She exited the pub, gasping for fresh air the moment the bandana found its way off her face. She could still taste the sugar, but it was getting less and less prominent as more time passed.

A sound of stubborn clicking grabbed her attention. She turned her head to find the source, spotting a man sitting on the steps of a barbershop, shining the shoes of a wealthy merchant. The merchant's leather shoes were more expensive than Dalia's outfit, her weapons, and the gold pieces that she still had left in her jacket pocket.

The merchant threw a coin at the shoe shiner as he walked away toward the coach waiting for him on the cobblestones nearby.

Dalia approached the shiner. "Hey, did you see what happened across the street at the pub?"

"Depends who's asking," the shiner replied, sizing up Dalia.

"Stop playing games and tell me what you know. I'm looking for two people—a girl with blonde hair and a boy with dark hair."

The shiner threw a smile at Dalia, sensing urgency and desperation in her voice. "I don't know. Maybe I did see something."

Dalia smirked and clenched her fists. "What's your price, shiner?"

"I could use some gold to feed two baby girls I have at home."

Dalia rolled her eyes as she threw a coin toward the shiner.

The coin landed flat in the man's palm. He raised it to eye level and placed it in his mouth. He ground his rotten teeth on the surface, making a squeaky noise.

"Very well," the shoe shiner said, satisfied with the coin's resilience. "A black carriage came earlier this evening, decorated with the beautiful golden designs of a dragon. A few tall men wearing masks and bottles on their backs threw something into the pub and later carried two people out."

"Did you see who they carried out?"

"I didn't see their faces because they had bags over their heads, but I did see something shiny on one of their wrists."

"Where did they take them?"

"That way." The shoe shiner pointed down the street that ran to the ocean. "They went in a hurry," he added. "Do you know who they are? I mean, these people with the masks?"

"None of your business," Dalia responded. "Just stick to your shining, and you better have two kids at home, or I'll hunt you down."

****

The rumble of the carriage on an uneven road surface, crushing rocks under its weight, awoke Roderick. It took him a bit to force his eyelids open because they were too heavy to lift. Everything around him was dark.

As he took a deep breath, a piece of cloth was sucked into his mouth. He coughed it out, panicky. His body kept bouncing off the cold, wooden floor each time the carriage hit a small pothole. He jiggled around, but his hands were tied to something behind his back and his legs were bound together tightly by a thick rope. There was no way out of those restraints.

He moved his head to the left to find a hint of light penetrating the cloth over his head. The outlines of two people sitting on a bench near him materialized. Neither of them paid any attention to him, concentrating on something in front of them.

He shifted left to right, and his hands rubbed against something soft and warm—someone's hands.

"Sofia," he spoke, but received no response.

A gurgling sound came from behind his back.

"Sofia, is that you?" Roderick asked.

"Yes, it's me," Sofia replied, sounding half-asleep.

"Thank the gods." Roderick exhaled. He shifted his body to the left, testing how far he could move and how tight the rope was wrapped around his wrists. "There's someone with us in the carriage," Roderick whispered. "I can see them through the cloth."

"What do you suggest we do?" Sofia asked. "Where do you think they are taking us?"

"I don't know, but it looks like they need us alive. That's always a good sign," Roderick answered. "I hope it's not like the last time in Tarin. If they wanted us dead, why didn't they just kill us then and there?"

****

Dalia was galloping in pursuit of Sofia and Roderick's captors. She had stolen a horse from a nearby pub. The moonlight illuminated the road in front of her, allowing her to see any potential troubles coming her way.

Her body was glued to the horse's neck while her hair whipped violently around in the relentless wind.

Dalia continued following the road, which was deeply marked with the fresh tracks of a carriage.

She arrived at the top of a hill. Two miles in the distance, a cloud of dust covered the sky above the landscape. "That must be them," Dalia mumbled, and she jammed her heels into the horse's ribs.

Despite the wind, Dalia kept her eyes open. In the distance, she spotted water, a shoreline, and a single docked ship. "Captain Stanislas Hollow," Dalia mumbled under her breath as she stared at the imposing ship in the distance.

Dalia closed the distance to the carriage as she neared the end of the road. She needed another two minutes to catch up to them.

In the distance, the cloud of dust formed by the carriage separated into several smaller clouds.

Moments later, arrows flew out of the lower cloud, heading her way.

She pulled out a small, circular object from her jacket and, with a push of a finger, the object turned into a shield. She placed it in front of her face, feeling the impact of four arrows bounce off the shield and fall to the ground. Her horse lost its footing. She moved the shield to find two arrows protruding from the horse's chest.

As the horse struggled with each step, they managed to push forward for another hundred yards before he finally succumbed to his wounds, bringing Dalia down with him.

As she got back up, two more arrows lodged into the ground right by her left foot. She scrambled and dove behind the horse's body for cover.

Several arrows found their way into the dead horse's back, barely missing Dalia's scalp. Then four riders, dressed in dark robes, with skulls and bones etched on their chests, jumped off their equally dark horses and landed on the ground, barely producing any sound. They aimed their bows and arrows in Dalia's direction, ready to fire.

The only thing keeping her alive was the motionless body of the horse. Two shadows appeared in the sand near her feet. The shadows grew in size rapidly.

Dalia pulled out two small blades from her waist and placed one in each hand. She picked up a small rock from the ground and threw it over her head. The moment the rock connected with the road behind, the shadows to her right changed their positions. She immediately pushed off to the right while keeping her body grounded. Dalia flung both knives simultaneously as the two assassins tried to reposition their bows to aim at the new threat. Both knives found their targets, and the two assassins collapsed to the ground, one tightly clutching his bow.

A hail of arrows hit the dead horse inches above Dalia's head, and at least one passed over her head, shuffling her hair in passing. The moment the last arrow flew by, Dalia had a fraction of a second to react before the other two assassins reloaded their bows.

Dalia rolled to the left and pulled two more blades from her waist. She somersaulted, sending two deadly blades toward the assassins. They fell, dead.

Dalia looked at her left shoulder, where a long cut exposed her flesh. "It's just a graze," she said, smiling.

She tore a piece of cloth from her tunic and wrapped it around her left shoulder. Then she kneeled next to the dead horse. "Thank you for your sacrifice. I wish it hadn't ended this way for you." Dalia placed her right palm over the horse's eyes and closed them.

She walked up to a horse belonging to one of the dead assassins and, with a little bit of convincing, managed to win him over. Dalia found herself on top of the beast, squeezing its sides with sheer ferocity to keep it under control.

Dalia and her new companion rushed toward the docked ship that stood a mile ahead of her. Dalia's eyes started to blur while blood continued to snake down her arm.

As she neared the shore, Dalia jumped off the horse and landed near the sand dune. Using it as cover, she watched as Sofia and Roderick were pushed onto the ship. Their heads were covered with dark hoods. When they reached the ship's deck, the anchors were lifted in a hurry. Within seconds, the ship gained altitude as the sound of thallium engines roared to life, leaving Dalia behind like a speck of dust in a sea of sand.

****

Onboard Stanislas Hollow's ship, Sofia and Roderick were manhandled by a group of rowdy men. They pushed them into heavy, wooden chairs deep below the ship's deck, and then the hoods were removed.

They were in a small room with a dresser and mirror and a small table. A bearded man stood next to Sofia. He wore a mask that looked like a breathing apparatus.

"Where are we? What is this?" Sofia demanded.

The man behind the mask stared at her as he leaned forward, parking his masked face two feet away from her face. He then lazily lifted his hands to remove the mask. With a hissing sound, the mask came free and revealed his face.

Sofia lunged back, looking at the man but wishing she had not. She wanted to close her eyes so she would not have to look at his face, or rather the absence of it, any longer. Yet, she did not want to show weaknesses. *What is he?* Sofia continued to stare into his eyes.

The man's face was red and mushy as if it had been recently burned. His eyes were of different colors—one black and one green. Neither of them looked straight at Sofia. His teeth were baby blue, clearly constructed out of thallium. His hands were made of a metal of some sort, not thallium. There was no way of telling how old he was . . . or how old *it* was.

"Welcome to my ship, Princess," the man spoke, his lips barely touching each other. "My name is Captain Stanislas Hollow. I'm the man who has the pleasure of delivering you to the queen." Stanislas unfolded a piece of cloth with Sofia's face on it, topped by the bold lettering of a wanted poster.

"I'm excited to meet you, Princess. Truthfully, I'll be more excited when I get the reward for your capture. You know, you are worth a lot of thallium, my dear. Don't take this personally, but we all have to find ways to survive in this ruthless world. As a matter of fact, I think you are lucky that I captured you because at least I have certain standards for prisoners—I don't kill them myself." Stanislas Hollow attempted to smile, but his lips could not stretch that far.

Stanislas pulled Sofia's origami box out of his jacket and placed it in front of his face. "Interesting box," Stanislas said as he opened the box, revealing paper animals. He pulled out a paper mouse and studied it a little deeper. "So many died for this," Stanislas said as he lifted the paper mouse high in the air. "Paper."

Stanislas released the paper mouse from his fingers. The paper animal drifted through the air until it fell on top of the dresser. Stanislas closed the box and tucked it into his jacket.

"I will leave you two for a few moments while I send a message of your capture to the queen. I promise to return so we can continue our little conversation."

"Conversation?" Sofia yelled. The moment she caught herself sounding hostile, Sofia lowered her tone. "I'm sorry, Captain. I hope we can figure something out here. We've got some gold on us. We could pay you in exchange for our release. Are you interested?"

"Gold?" Stanislas spoke as the word lingered on his lips a little longer. "Interesting proposal," he said. "How much gold are we talking about here?"

"A lot," Sofia answered. "More than the queen can offer."

Captain Stanislas stood there, studying Sofia's convincing face, but he remained shy of making any deals with her. "I'm intrigued by your offer, I have to admit. I will thoroughly consider it. Until then, I will leave you in the company of one of my men. Until next time, Princess."

The captain left the room with one of his men, leaving one burly man behind to guard them.

CHAPTER 16

Dalia rode the horse to the *Sky Serpent*, disembarking it in a gallop near the dock. "Get the ship ready *now!*" she screamed at her puzzled crew, who were staring at her from the ship.

It took them a moment to realize she was serious. Then the cluster of men scrambled.

One of Dalia's lieutenants approached her in a hurry. "Captain, we still have some men left in the city. What do we do with them?"

"Rozen, send someone to find them. They have exactly fifteen minutes to return to the ship, or we leave without them."

The lieutenant sent two of his fastest and youngest into the city to herd the men. Then he joined the rest of the crew to make final preparations for a takeoff.

The word spread like a brush fire among the men left in the city. No one wanted to stay behind and lose their chance of getting a large payout. Despite the gallons of liquor they'd downed in the last several hours, the men ran back to the ship as if their lives depended on it.

The ship's engines howled while the sails inflated upward. Men at the pulleys worked hard to lift the ship's four anchors into the air. The ship was afloat within minutes.

"Head northwest!" Dalia yelled to the man behind the stern. "I want to catch up to Stanislas's ship by sunrise. I don't care how or where. I want someone to find me that damned ship!"

The *Sky Serpent*'s engines worked overtime as the ship flew at high speed. The wind was favorable, too, giving them an extra push.

Dalia kept pacing back and forth on the main deck, irritated. She squeezed her blade's grip, which rested flush against her thighs, until the pain stopped her from squeezing it any further. "I can't believe I was this naïve," Dalia scolded herself.

****

Hours later, when the sun was about to appear in the sky, someone yelled, "The ship! I see the ship!"

Dalia grabbed a retractable telescope, extended it, and placed it against her right eye. "That's the one. We got them!"

Dalia ordered her men to cut the power to the engine by half and to inflate the sails to bring them higher up. "Let's use the cover of the clouds to approach them from above. The only way this will work is if we surprise them," Dalia told her men.

With remnants of the night as their ally, the *Sky Serpent* floated through the air above its target.

Dalia grew nervous. She was counting on a surprise attack, but the chances of them not noticing her ship were slim to none.

When the *Sky Serpent* was right above the target ship, Dalia approached her navigating officer. "I need you to come down a bit, but make sure you don't hit the mainmast."

Six of her crew stood by her side, ready to board the enemy ship at her command.

"Remember, men, the mission is to rescue Sofia and Roderick, not kill the enemy and take over the ship. It's about silence and precision. Understood?"

"Aye, Captain!" the men spoke in unison.

Four other crewmembers stood by the side of the ship, struggling with two heavy ropes in their hands. They were thick and long enough to reach the enemy ship.

Dalia looked at the ship operator, who studied a device resembling a compass. He waved, advising her that the ship was on top of their target. The only hope Dalia had was that the other ship had not seen them coming.

"It's time," Dalia spoke, giving her crew a signal to throw the ropes overboard. Then Dalia, followed by six other men, jumped onto the ropes and slid down into the carpet of clouds.

Dalia was the first to emerge below the cloud cover and noticed that her rope hung above some containers on the ship's front end. The other rope landed on the floor of the ship, not far from the containers. It looked like a ghost ship, too quiet and too easy for her liking.

Dalia and three of her crew landed safely on top of the containers while the other three landed on the main deck below them. They climbed down the containers and joined the other three.

"Let's move toward the captain's quarters. That is the most likely place they would keep prisoners of such importance to the queen," Dalia whispered.

Dalia turned to face Rozen. "I need you to stay here and alert the *Sky Serpent* if you sense any trouble. If we don't come out within five minutes, raise the alarm."

"Aye, Captain! May the gods be with you."

The intruders moved swiftly toward the other end of the ship. It was eerie how quiet it was. Not a single soul in sight. Even the wind had stopped blowing. Dalia could only hear her steady breathing and the breaths of a man standing beside her.

When they reached the door, Dalia counted down from five with her right hand. When she closed her hand into a fist, she grabbed the doorknob and turned it clockwise. The door swung open.

They went in silently, finding themselves in a hallway with a glow of orange lights coming from two side rooms, which appeared to be open.

Dalia and her men stormed into one of the rooms with their weapons out, expecting resistance on the other end. All they found was an empty room.

A sudden *thud,* followed by the violent shaking of the ship, sent everyone to the ground. Dalia grabbed a table that stood in the middle of the room. Moments later, it found its way to the farthest corner, with Dalia still clutching one of its legs.

"What was that?" one of the crewmen asked.

"Whatever it was, it can't be good," Dalia answered.

As they regained their composure and moved from the commander's quarters and onto the ship's deck, they realized the violent shaking had come from above.

Moments later, the motionless body of one of her crewmen fell three feet away from where she stood, breaking two planks on the ship's deck.

Before she was able to say anything, another body fell through the clouds, landing several feet farther down. This one, however, had a knife protruding from his chest.

"My gods, we are under attack!" Dalia scrambled to climb up the rope.

A large number of pirates had reached the deck of the *Sky Serpent* from above, where they engaged in vicious fighting with Dalia's crew. They had the element of surprise on their side, which clearly showed the difference on the battlefield. Another advantage was that their enemy was leaderless and their ranks were in disarray. The battle was becoming a bloodbath.

Dalia's men were falling to their deaths one by one. Something needed to change, and it had to be done fast or everything would be lost.

Dalia climbed the rope toward *Sky Serpent* as her men rained from above. The chaos around her ensued. The body of her trusted officer flew past her, landing on thc wooden crates several feet below.

"Captain," the officer forced the word out. "I'm sorry. They surprised us," he said as he gasped for air, which never reached his lungs.

Dalia shook her head and pulled out a curved blade as she continued ascending toward her ship to join the fight.

****

On the ship above the *Sky Serpent*, inside a small room, Sofia and Roderick sat tied together to their chairs. Their hands were tied at their wrists while their arms sat numbly in their laps. One burly man stood guard, watching them closely. His shaved head glistened in the light produced by a naphtha lamp on the dresser, which sat several feet in front of Sofia. The man's dirty hands were bigger than Sofia's head.

She eyed his blade, which was close to her yet still way out of her reach. The blade rested on the man's belt, flanked by two smaller knives.

When Stanislas had left them alone with his burly gorilla, Sofia had looked around the room for anything she could use to escape from the place. The first thing that popped into her mind was the paper mouse resting on top of the dresser. She could not believe the captain was that reckless as to leave it there. She also knew this was not the time, or place, to argue the captain's decision, which would only help her cause.

What if he left it there on purpose to provoke us into an escape? If that's the case, what would he gain?

An idea of escape entered Sofia's mind as she stared at the mouse. The only obstacle to her plan was the burly pirate staring at her. *This is not going to work. How am I supposed to fight this guy when we are tied up?*

Her blank stare into the mirror showed a girl who once had everything figured out. She looked for a sign of old Sofia, but that girl was gone. Now she was Elan, Princess of Thalia.

As she closed her eyes, her body shivered at the sound of cannons firing and the ship shaking. Sofia opened her eyes at the sound of voices outside the cabin.

The gorilla man looked at Sofia and then at the door. Then, without a word said, he departed the cabin in a hurry.

They were finally alone.

Sofia turned her attention to Roderick. "Hey, are you awake?" she asked.

"As awake as one can be," Roderick professed.

"Okay. We need to move together so I can reach the dresser. They left the paper mouse out in the open. I might be able to reach for it to free us if I can get closer to it."

“That sounds good,” Roderick said.

“Tell me when to move. We need to do it at the same time,” Sofia told him. “Let’s move on the count of three.”

“One . . . two . . . three.”

Roderick and Sofia used all their strength to move a couple of inches closer to the dresser. Despite the push, they were still too far from their final destination. It took several more pushes before Sofia felt confident she was close enough.

“I think this is close enough,” she said, sounding out of breath.

“How do you plan on reaching the paper mouse?” Roderick asked, shifting in his chair.

“I’ll blow at it.”

“Blow at it? If you blow it, you will only push it farther away,” Roderick said.

“Maybe true, but there is nothing else that comes to my mind. I hope by blowing at it, it will fall to the floor and I can then pick it up.”

“How do you intend to do that?” Roderick asked.

“That depends on where it lands on the floor,” Sofia responded.

Sofia looked at the paper mouse on the dresser and filled her lungs with air that she feared would kill the flame in the naphtha lamp, which sat beside the paper creature. She let the air out in the direction of the paper mouse. The air pushed the paper mouse closer to the edge. The flame burning in the lamp swayed back and forth and was on the verge of going out.

“Did you make it?” Roderick asked.

"Not yet, but close," Sofia sighed. "I think I'll give it another try. We should move to the right so I can get closer to it."

The two of them moved once more in unison. With two jolts to the right, Sofia knew they had moved far enough. She filled her lungs with nasty, humid air and readied herself for another blow.

One more exhale pushed the paper mouse off the dresser and onto the floor.

"It worked! It worked!" Sofia proclaimed.

Roderick smiled, though Sofia could not see it.

"Now what?" he asked.

"Let's move a little more to the right, and then we must tip the chairs over, so I can land on my face."

"You want to tip the chairs so you can land on your face?"

"Precisely," Sofia said. "If I fall on top of the mouse, I might be able to get ahold of it with my hand and release its power. Then I can get on top of us in the mouse form to bite the rope."

Roderick nodded his head as they moved in unison to the right, tipping the chairs over and sending Sofia to the floor, with Roderick on top of her.

Sofia managed to move her head to the side so she would not fall directly on her nose. The last thing she needed was a broken nose. However, the weight of Roderick on top of her put a strain on Sofia's chest, making it hard to breathe.

She had fallen short of her target, which now lay about a foot from her hands.

Sofia repositioned her head slightly downward and blew enough air in the direction of the paper mouse. The air pushed the mouse closer to her hands but still not close enough. Struggling with the pressure and weight of Roderick on top of her, Sofia gasped for more air. The paper mouse fluttered and lifted into the air and was about to escape from beneath her body when she managed to seize it.

"I got it!" she exclaimed.

She shuffled the origami in her hands until it reached her right hand, and then Sofia released it from her grip. A sense of weightlessness overtook her body as she saw herself lying in an awkward position on the floor. At the same time, Roderick stared up at the ceiling, unable to do anything.

Sofia moved swiftly in her new body, climbing up her leg until she reached the rope, which kept them both tied together. She chewed on it, which took much longer than she had anticipated. Roderick freed himself and rolled off her back. The mouse returned to Sofia's right palm, and his wiggly tail transformed into a paper tail.

Sofia and Roderick looked around the room for the rest of their stuff but could not find anything. Then Roderick opened the door to take a peek at what waited for them on the other side. Yelling came from farther down the hall, followed by some loud explosions.

"I can't see anyone around," he said, not sounding too confident. "Are you ready to go?"

"I can't leave without the knife and the magic paper. We need to find them first," Sofia said, voicing her frustration.

Roderick nodded.

Unease overtook Sofia. *This was too easy.* She looked down at her hands and noticed they were shaking. She clenched both fists to stop the trembling as they went down a tight hallway, following the sound of explosions.

On their way out, they faced two doors, one on each side of the hallway.

"We need to check these rooms before we leave," Sofia said.

Before they were able to choose the door, the ship shook violently, sending Roderick into the door on the right side of the hallway. As his body connected with the door, it swung open, and Roderick found himself inside. Sofia was right behind him.

The room stretched about forty feet, with a long table in the middle that was surrounded by chairs of different sizes and shapes. It looked like a conference room or maybe a dining room for the top brass. There was not much there to search through other than an armoire standing against one of the walls.

They approached the armoire and opened it. It contained a porcelain dining set and tea cups that were neatly stacked and reinforced by wooden crates to protect them from the ship's rocking.

"This is clearly a dining room," Roderick said.

"At least they keep everything nice and tidy," Sofia remarked.

Roderick turned his gaze to Sofia, smiling at her comment. "It's good to see that you care about the cleanliness of the people who kidnapped us."

Sofia smiled in return, then turned around to face the door that they had just come through. "Let's check out the other room."

They crossed the short hallway and entered the other room unopposed. As they walked in, the door behind them closed.

Both turned around to find one of the burly pirates from their holding room standing behind them, blocking their only way out.

"Looks like someone else is very interested in you, Princess," Captain Stanislas Hollow spoke from behind them. "They dared to attack me. But I outsmarted them when we switched the ships and used the other one as bait. This fight can only end one way—with my victory!"

Roderick and Sofia turned around and saw a chair behind a large mahogany desk. On the middle of the desk sat Sofia's box and Roderick's belt. The chair swung around, revealing Captain Hollow.

He held the Knife of Life in his hands. "I wondered if what the royal court said about you was true."

"And what is it that they said?" Sofia asked.

"They said you are dangerous and that you possess magic. I can only assume you freed yourselves thanks to your magical power? I left the paper mouse there on purpose to witness this myself. It's not as if you could harm me in your mouse form."

No response came from either Sofia or Roderick.

"See," the captain continued, pulling out a flintlock pistol from behind his desk, "this pistol fires thallium bullets. Your magic doesn't stand a chance against it. All I need is one shot, and you are dead, so I suggest you not try anything stupid. I also suggest you help me with something in exchange for your friend's life," Stanislas Hollow said, pointing the pistol at Roderick. "I want you to use your creatures for me. You see, I enjoy breaking the rules. The royal court wants you dead or alive, but I think I could benefit from you more if I don't hand you over. What do you say?"

Sofia looked at Roderick for an answer but found nothing useful. He stood cemented to the floor, expressionless.

Sofia turned back to face Stanislas. "If I agree to help you, will you spare Roderick's life?"

Stanislas burped as he shifted in the chair. "Ha, you are not in a position to negotiate. We both know if you transform into one of those things, your body will stay paralyzed, so don't test me. If I want to, I could force one of those creatures into your palm, and you would be under my control until I start feeling some compassion," Captain Hollow said, tapping his pistol. "Just so I make myself clear, we are not negotiating here. You *will* help me by doing jobs I ask you to do in exchange for your life and the life of this boy here." The captain once again pointed his pistol at Roderick.

Sofia did not like the offer but was not ready to say no to Captain Hollow. She wanted to buy more time to come up with a plan to get out of this situation.

"I need your answer now," Captain Hollow demanded.

"I don't think I can do that," Sofia said. "I need assurances that Roderick will live."

"You stupid child!" Captain Hollow yelled, then signaled to his bodyguard to seize Roderick.

The pirate grabbed Roderick, squeezing his arms by his sides.

Captain Hollow laughed, enjoying himself. While he was busy laughing, Sofia discreetly took the paper mouse from her front tunic pocket and released it from her palm. The mouse ran up to the pirate's feet and bit his right ankle. The pirate screamed and reached for his injured ankle, allowing Roderick to seize the knife hanging at the pirate's waist. The knife found its way deep into the pirate's chest before Captain Hollow could react.

Captain Hollow lifted his right hand and aimed the pistol at Roderick, who managed to slip behind the dead pirate. The bullet lodged itself in the pirate's body. The captain aimed again, and as he fired, Roderick pushed the dead pirate forward. The body knocked the desk into Captain Hollow's gut. The impact forced the captain to drop the pistol as he gasped for air.

As he scrambled to get ahold of the pistol, Sofia climbed onto the desk in her mouse form and bit Stanislas's right thumb, eliciting a scream.

"You little . . ." Stanislas yelled, shaking his hand. Stanislas then made another attempt for the pistol, but before he could reach it, his entire body jerked backward.

He looked down at the knife embedded in his chest. Then he looked up at Roderick, who stood with his arm outstretched, holding the knife. Captain Stanislas Hollow took one more deep breath before his chest stopped rising and falling.

"We need to go," Roderick stated. He picked up his belt and collapsible bow from the dead captain's desk.

Sofia reentered to her human self, then took the Knife of Life from the captain, along with the box of magic paper lying on the desk.

CHAPTER 17

On the ship's main deck, Sofia and Roderick found chaos erupting all around them. Pirates were running around, throwing bombs overboard. Many of them jumped onto the ropes that hung on the opposite side of the ship. Near the starboard of the ship, a bomb exploded, sending two of the pirates into the air.

Roderick and Sofia crouched behind the largest of several wooden crates peppering the ship's deck. Several heavy ropes hung nearby.

Roderick peeked overboard to find people fighting on the main deck of the *Sky Serpent* below.

"What's going on?" Sofia asked.

"It looks like our captors attacked the *Sky Serpent*. I can't tell who has the upper hand, but if I had to guess, I think Dalia is losing the battle."

Sofia looked overboard at the chaos, scanning the ship for any sign of Dalia. She could not find her. There were so many people down there. Like ants, they moved around the ship. It was impossible to tell who was who.

Sofia retreated to the safety of the wooden crates.

Then Roderick's eyes grew as wide. "Watch out!" he yelled as he pushed Sofia aside and pulled his short blade from around his waist. He thrust the blade upward, burying it into the chest of a pirate leaping over a wooden crate.

The pirate's heavy body fell on top of Roderick.

"Roderick!" Sofia screamed. She pushed the pirate off him. Roderick lay on his back, his chest covered in blood. "My God, you're bleeding!" She grabbed his shirt, looking for the entrance wound to stop the bleeding.

Roderick looked at her, seemingly calm. "It's okay. It's not my blood."

Sofia met his eyes and caught a smirk forming on his face. She turned her attention to the pirate's body, where the handle of Roderick's small blade protruded from his chest.

"I hate you!" she screamed as she punched Roderick on his uninjured shoulder. "I thought I lost you."

Roderick blushed, then cleared his throat. "We need to get onto one of those ropes and off this ship."

"Lead the way," Sofia said, fixing her hair.

They slid down the rope toward Dalia's wounded ship. The chaos became more intense as they approached.

"Stay close to me when we get down!" Roderick yelled over the explosions and fighting raging around them.

"Got it!"

The moment Roderick's feet met the wooden deck of the *Sky Serpent*, he was charged from the right by an angry pirate.

"Watch your right!" Sofia yelled, still clutching the rope above him.

Roderick twisted to avoid the pirate's sharp sword. He used the momentum of the pirate's charge to push him overboard and into the clouds below.

“Thank you,” he managed to say as he helped Sofia from the rope.

“We need to look for Dalia,” Sofia said as they moved toward a spot where they could observe the entire ship. They climbed onto a wooden crate full of potatoes and peeked between them.

It was obvious that things were not going well for Dalia’s crew. Many of her men lay motionless on the ground while the farthest part of the ship was ablaze. They could not see Dalia.

“Where is she? Can you see her?” Sofia asked.

“I can’t see her anywhere,” Roderick replied.

“What do we do now?”

“Follow me,” Roderick said. They moved behind another set of wooden crates full of Kari fruit.

Several feet away, toward the edge of the ship, two ropes hung overboard. Roderick moved quickly, looking down where the two ropes disappeared into the clouds below.

“What’s that?” Sofia asked.

“I have to say that I’m just as puzzled,” Roderick answered.

“Are they abandoning the ship?” Sofia asked.

“To go where?” Roderick replied.

“To . . .”

Before Sofia could come up with a guess, a man emerged from the cloud below Roderick. It was one of Dalia’s officers.

Roderick’s eyes met him.

“Roderick, you’re alive! We went down to rescue you. It’s a trap. The captain is in trouble. You must help.”

Before he could share any more information, an arrow struck the officer’s neck, sending him to his death.

“Dalia must still be down there,” Roderick gasped.

“We must help her.” Sofia felt guilt for all that was happening around them. *How many people must die because of me?*

She pulled her wooden box from her tunic, grabbing the paper eagle out of it.

“Keep me safe, and I’ll do the rest,” Sofia said as she released the eagle from her hand, not waiting for Roderick’s approval.

Sofia found herself in the air, looking at Roderick down below, crouching next to her motionless body. It was a fantastic feeling of power and freedom.

She retracted her wings to her body as she went into a dive. She cut through the clouds with ease, and when she reached the bottom, she found Dalia suspended in the air on one of the ropes, engaged in a sword fight with an enemy pirate. Right above them, another pirate hung on the rope. On the rope next to hers, one of Dalia’s men fought another pirate. He looked gravely hurt and would not last much longer. Before she made a whole loop around the ship, Dalia’s man had already fallen to his death.

Dalia was high in the air now, facing two dangers—one from two attacking pirates and one from falling to her death. There was only one feasible option in Sofia’s mind. She must attack the pirates to give Dalia a chance at survival.

The second pirate, who moments ago had killed Dalia’s man, swayed on his rope, preparing to attack Dalia from the right. Her death was nothing but imminent.

Sofia climbed up to gain speed, and then she dived toward the pirate swaying on the rope next to Dalia. Instinctively, Sofia pushed her talons out as she approached the swaying pirate. She grabbed his chest and managed to lift him, dislodging him from the rope. Then she opened her talons and let the pirate fall to his death thousands of feet below. It was a moment of realization for Sofia.

I killed a man to save Dalia. What does that make me?

It was not easy to comprehend the complexity of her feelings or the lack thereof. *Does this make me a murderer or a savior?* Sofia had entered a different territory of human emotions.

Does this mean my demon returned with a vengeance? Sofia's eagle eyes met Dalia's desperate eyes. For a moment, Sofia thought Dalia recognized her in her eagle form.

Dalia held on to the rope tightly, but Sofia could tell her palms were burning. Sofia had to do something to help. Luckily, a decision was not hard to make, especially after her first official kill. Therefore, she decided she must kill more pirates so she could save the one person she cared about . . . a person she owed her life to.

Sofia pulled back and flew up again to gain momentum. Then she aimed herself at the pirate above Dalia. Once again, her talons connected with the man's flesh, pulling him away from the rope while he hung tightly to it.

Sofia's eagle body was too powerful for the pirate, who was already exhausted from fighting Dalia. He gave up, but not because Sofia was pulling on him; Dalia's blade had cut through his stomach. Moments later, the man fell to his sky grave.

The pirate who hung on the rope above descended rapidly.

As Sofia pulled back up to ready herself for another attack, her eyes met Dalia's for a moment. Sofia could swear Dalia sent her an approving wink as she continued to ascend toward the *Sky Serpent*.

Moments later, Dalia's face contorted as she looked up toward the pirate above her. He was cutting the rope between him and Dalia. Dalia's life was hanging on two or three threads.

Sofia had no other option than to grab Dalia with her talons, but she was afraid she would not be able to hold her weight. *I need to get her to the safety of her ship.* Sofia descended Dalia's way.

Another thread broke, followed by another. The rope snapped with Dalia still clutching it, and she went into a freefall.

Sofia rushed her way, but it was too late. For a second, she forgot to flap her wings.

As the blood returned to her brain, Sofia knew she had another option. *Hopefully, it's not too late.* She flew upward, cutting through the thick clouds. She was stunned at the sight of herself and Roderick standing in the same spot where she had left them. Shortly after, Sofia returned to her human self.

Roderick's heart pounded heavily when Sofia returned to her body, but the moment lasted less than two seconds before Sofia reached into her origami box and pulled out the paper dragon.

"No time to explain," she said.

She picked it up and tried to force her mind to concentrate. *You can do this. You must help Dalia. You must do the right thing.*

Sofia managed to clear her mind of all thoughts and emotions as she concentrated her entire energy on the dragon origami in her palm. She released it from her palm, and an invigorating strength rushed through her body. Her body rose into the air as the sound of large, flapping wings resonated in her ears. She opened her eyes to find herself ascending into the sky above the ship. Sofia was a dragon, and the dragon was Sofia.

The dragon's heartbeat was loud. It intensified in an instant as Sofia remembered why she had transformed into it in the first place.

After several seconds of gliding in the air, the air density around her changed as she moved downward like an arrow, reaching extreme speeds. In the far distance, below the cloud cover, a dark speck appeared. With nothing else in sight, Sofia went for it, hoping it was Dalia's falling body. She glanced to the left and right to see if she could see any other specks in the distance, but nothing caught her sharp dragon sight.

Sofia raced downward, and as she got closer, she feared she was too late to save Dalia. The water below was rushing towards them. At the same time, the speck in the distance turned into a human body, bearing Dalia's face. She appeared peaceful.

Sofia made a final push, straining her dragon's wings and muscles. *I must win this race. I must save Dalia.* For once, Sofia wanted to save someone's life. She had failed at saving her father or Luna. *I must save her, or all of this was for nothing.*

As she cut through the air like a razor blade, she repositioned her body, preparing for impact with the water. Sofia extended her legs as she came close to Dalia's motionless body. Before Dalia hit the water, Sofia managed to grab her, clutching her between her claws. Then Sofia rapidly flapped her wings to slow herself down, the bottom of her wings grazing the water's surface. With a last push of her dragon strength, Sofia fought the resistance of gravity as she climbed back up. *I did it!*

There was something satisfying about saving a human life. . . Saving Dalia's life. She savored the moment of her accomplishment and courage as she flew upward. *Now we are even.*

She glanced at Dalia. Her body was bent unnaturally, with arms outstretched toward the water. Sofia prayed that Dalia would live another day to return to the land of the living. *Please stay alive. We are almost there.* Sofia returned to the *Sky Serpent* to find Roderick finishing off two pirates who had charged him from the left. She landed next to him, placing Dalia's body next to her own with utmost care. She then surveyed the ship and could see the situation was dire for Dalia's men.

She lifted herself into the sky above the ship and released a fiery inferno on the ropes, stretching upward to the pirate ship that had once held her hostage. About a dozen enemy pirates burned to their deaths, still clutching the ropes.

Sofia did another sweep above the ship, during which she grabbed several enemy pirates with her claws, dumping them overboard and to their deaths. With her help, Dalia's men found renewed strength to overcome the attacking pirates and save their ship from its certain demise.

In a rage, Sofia flew to the enemy ship that was trying to flee. She turned it into ashes. The feeling in her chest was hard to explain. She did not feel sorry for the terror that she cast upon those on the burning ship. Sofia might have killed many men that day, but she also saved many. Most importantly, she had saved one life worth saving.

****

Several hours passed before Dalia finally opened her eyes. Sofia sat by her side.

"What happened?" Dalia asked.

"Just rest, we can talk about it later."

"My entire body hurts," she moaned.

"I'm not surprised," Sofia said. "You've been through a lot."

Dalia looked at her. "Wait… I was… I fell from the rope and was falling through the clouds, plunging toward the ground. That was the last thing I remember." She shook her head and began to push her legs off the bed. "I need to get out to check on my men."

"Take it easy," Sofia said, grabbing Dalia's arm.

"I don't need help getting out of bed," Dalia said, pushing herself off the bed onto her unsteady feet.

Sofia followed Dalia to the main deck. Her men, or what was left of them, helped each other with their wounds or worked on extinguishing several small fires that lingered.

"Is Roderick OK?" Dalia asked, turning toward Sofia just as Roderick appeared from the other side.

"Well, look who is up and walking," Roderick said, looking at Dalia.

A smile formed on Dalia's face. "You're alive?"

"Surprised to see me in one piece?" Roderick asked.

"That's not what I—"

"I'm just kidding," Roderick interrupted. "I'm glad to see you're up and in one piece, too."

Dalia made a labored step forward. "What happened? I remember falling, and then I remember nothing more. How . . .? How did I end up here?"

"You are alive, thanks to Sofia," Roderick said, turning in Sofia's direction. "She turned into a dragon and managed to rescue you. My gods, it was a majestic sight to behold."

Dalia looked at Roderick and then turned toward Sofia. "I see," she said.

"What about Hollow's ship?" Dalia asked.

"That ship is no more," Roderick replied. "Thanks to Sofia, the dragon. She burned that hunk of wood to ashes."

****

The trip to the capital was long and, thankfully, uneventful. The *Sky Serpent* made several stops along the way to restock supplies and fix what had to be fixed. This gave Dalia and Roderick time to heal.

"How's your shoulder doing?" Sofia asked as she sat next to Roderick.

"Oh, it feels great. I don't feel any pain anymore. That ointment Dalia picked up in Portal City made a huge difference.

"I don't want to bore you with my questions," Roderick said. "But tell me more about this world of yours. I want to know more about those things you call cars. Everything seems so fascinating."

Sofia smiled. "Cars are these things that people drive on the roads to transport them to places. They use engines that run on gasoline, similar to thallium, just in a liquid state."

"In a liquid state? That sounds weird. How is that even possible?"

Sofia laughed wholeheartedly. "Really? You think that's weird, but flying ships are not?"

Roderick blushed again. "I'm sorry if I brought up the wrong topic. I just wanted to learn more about you. I watched you growing up in that bed, unable to move, unable to talk. Now

I finally sit next to you in flesh and blood, and I feel like I want to know everything about you—how you felt during all those years in a coma, did you see us, hear us . . ."

Sofia shifted her gaze downward. "I . . . I didn't sleep, Roderick. It's hard for me to explain this to you, especially when I'm confused about it. I don't know what to believe anymore. My life is like a Ferris wheel in a free spin. It keeps running in circles."

Sofia looked up into the sky, trying to fight the tears forming in her eyes. "Losing my father was the toughest thing I have ever experienced. He was my engine of positivity. I was always self-aware of my shortcomings, but he was there to remind me of how beautiful I am. He always found a way to switch something negative to something positive," Sofia said as she let out a short laugh.

"Y-You *are* beautiful," Roderick stuttered out.

"Thank you, Roderick. That means a lot to me." She gave him a soft smile. "Secretly, I wish all *this* was real. At moments, when I wake up, I refuse to open my eyes, fearing what I'm going to find on the other side. I don't know what I want more—to see my mom and return to my old life of misery or stay here to be hunted by the queen but have you around."

Roderick lowered his head, looking down at his feet. "I wish I could switch places with you to offer you better choices, but my life is also far from perfect. Sometimes, I wish I had a different upbringing and had my parents and brother around."

"Brother?" Sofia said, raising her eyebrows.

"His name was Veli," Roderick said. "He was my twin brother. He died during birth, together with our mother. For a long time, I blamed myself for their deaths, and I still do."

Sofia placed her hand on Roderick's shoulder. "Don't. You can't blame yourself. You had nothing to do with their deaths, and I bet they would be proud of you for what you accomplished and the kind of person you've turned out to be."

Roderick faced Sofia, who now stood shoulder-to-shoulder with him. "Thank you for your kind words, Princess. They mean more to me than you can imagine.

"My entire life revolved around training and preparing for what has taken place in the past several weeks. I might be sad about my early life, but I can't be happier about how things are going in the present. I am happy to be able to stand by your side and have a conversation with you.

"I used to sit by your bed often, reading to you. On many occasions, when Master Fry would leave the cabin, I would share stories like this with you. It made me feel better. You were always there for me. Even though you don't remember any of it, I want you to know that you kept me going. You kept me alive."

Sofia's eyes filled with tears for both of them—two teenagers from two different worlds who'd shared the misfortune of losing a parent at an early age.

She looked at Roderick, who was staring at the sky. She replaced her hand on Roderick's shoulder with her head, and they both continued to stare into the vastness of the sky, wishing for a better future.

CHAPTER 18

Under the veil of darkness, the *Sky Serpent* found a dark alcove not far from the capital to dock. The crew lowered a small boat into the water below. Roderick, Sofia, Dalia, and one crewman boarded it quickly. With stable and precise motions of his hands, Dalia's sailor pulled a metallic crank attached to the engine, which hummed in protest as it came to life. The boat then propelled toward the city.

The trip to the capital was smooth and uneventful. The sailor used a lever to steer the boat as it glided across the sea. The lights of the capital became more visible in the distance as the thick layer of clouds above them broke apart, giving way to the bright, full moon.

The capital looked impressive from the water. A large castle stood on top of a rock, stretching above the lower city, which was reserved for the less fortunate. The Cathedral of Souls stood prominently in the center of the city, like a giant surrounded by hundreds of dwarfs.

The vessel carrying the four passengers approached the makeshift harbor in the slums of the capital, away from the all-seeing eyes of the royal guard.

This part of the capital was dirty, rundown, and dark but full of life. At all hours of the day or night, people strolled down the uninviting streets, looking for something to help them survive another day.

The stench of the garbage on the streets made Sofia gag. They passed rotten rodent carcasses stacked up next to a butcher shop. *I hope they don't use that meat to make sausages.* Sofia pinched her nose to stop the stench from invading her delicate nostrils.

As they continued navigating the streets of the lower capital, Dalia cut through alleys with pure confidence. She clearly knew these streets like the insides of her pockets.

Dalia led them toward Bartholomeu's house with ease. Roderick had shared this information with her during their trip to the capital.

"It's not far from here," Dalia said, breaking a long silence.

As they turned yet another corner in the never-ending maze of small buildings and rundown shacks, they stopped abruptly when Dalia swooped her arm up in a stopping motion.

"That's the place right there." She pointed toward a small shack, no bigger or smaller than any of its neighbors. "I will let you two do your thing while I catch up on all the rumors I missed since I left the slums. If you need me, you can find me in one of the pubs not far away from here."

Dalia turned around without making any eye contact and left in the same direction that they had come from.

Dalia's sudden departure felt a little odd to Sofia, who looked at Roderick and shrugged her shoulders. Her curiosity about Dalia quickly dissipated as her attention turned to the small shack in front of her.

The shack had four windows visible from the street. All were covered by heavy wooden shutters, not allowing any light to enter or leave the house. The only sign of life was a dim light shining from under the front door.

They inched toward the door, looking left and right while crossing the street.

As they moved closer, Roderick lifted his arm to knock. But Sofia grabbed him.

"Wait," she whispered. "This doesn't look right. Look at the bottom of the door. Edgar said that Bartholomeu lives alone, but I just saw two shadows pass by in the same direction."

Roderick looked down as two shadows moved to the left of the door, one following the other.

"I suggest we get back to the safety of the alley so we can think this through," Roderick whispered back.

As they watched the shack from the semi-safety of the dark alley across the street, Sofia said, "I have an idea." She pulled the small wooden box of origami from her tunic as Roderick crossed his arms.

"What are you doing?"

"I'm going in to see what's waiting for us on the other side," she replied with a wide smile. Then she shifted the paper origami in the box until she found what she was looking for—the paper bat.

She closed the wooden box, placed it back into her pocket, and without another word, relaxed her body and mind as she released the paper bat into the air.

The paper bat transformed into a real bat, flapping its wings and flying in circles above the alley. Sofia's frozen body stood next to Roderick, unsettling and disturbing but still beautiful.

The bat flew higher into the sky, hovered above the chimney of Bartholomeu's cabin for several seconds, and then dove through it without any fear of what was waiting on the other end.

Sofia landed at the bottom of the chimney on a piece of charcoal as dark as her bat body. She surveyed the interior of the cabin from the new vantage point and spotted a frail, old man with a long, white beard tied up to a chair with a thick piece of cloth stuffed in his mouth. He wore a piece of gray cloth around his waist.

That must be Bartholomeu. Sofia then shifted her attention toward the front door. There stood three royal guardsmen, patiently waiting for someone's arrival. Hers perhaps?

This was clearly not a welcoming party. Two rifles leaned against the wall facing the street where Roderick stood with her human body. One of the men had a pistol at his waist.

A thudding noise brought a fourth man into Sofia's view. He came from an adjacent room, which was why she had not originally seen him. He positioned himself right in front of the fireplace, where Sofia stared at his broad thighs.

One of the men broke the awkward silence that had overtaken the cabin since her arrival.

"Sir, do you think they are coming?" the man closest to the rifles spoke.

The man standing in front of Sofia responded in a monotone voice, "Patience, boys. Our source said they should be here shortly." As the boss guard spoke, he moved away from the fireplace and approached Bartholomeu.

Source? What is he talking about? Does this mean someone followed us here? Sofia's bat brain felt too small to process the rapid influx of information. She thought about a possible traitor, about poor Bartholomeu and how to save him, and about Roderick with her human body. There was a lot to think about and not enough time.

Sofia shook off all those thoughts and focused on how to deal with the situation in front of her. She looked for weaknesses and only found one—the rifles leaning against the wall on the other side of the room. They had a flintlock mechanism operated by a speck of thallium.

Another look at the soldiers near the door revealed they only had blades as their side weapons, so she determined that the two rifles most likely belonged to those two. *I should disable those rifles, which will buy us some time when we get through that door. But how?*

Sofia tried to remember from history books and old movies how flintlock rifles operated. The only problem was thallium with its baby blue glow. *How do I disable thallium?*

There was only one way to find out—fly to the rifles and check them out. It was not like Sofia knew how the flint rifle should operate, but she understood the concept.

Sofia waited until the soldiers engaged in another conversation before she flew across the room, flapping her wings as fast as she could and landing on the floor beneath the rifles. Her body blended in with the dark stock of the rifle that cast its shadow on the floor, giving Sofia some extra concealment.

Her flyby had not gone unnoticed. One of the soldiers turned around, sensing some movement.

"Did you see that?" he asked the other two.

"See what," one of the soldiers asked. "A ghost?"

The two soldiers burst out laughing. The third shrugged them off

Sofia waited another ten seconds or so before she climbed up the body of the rifle until she reached the firing mechanism. She examined the rifle. It was clear that the flint was used to strike a small speck of thallium, making black powder nonessential to fire the weapon. Sofia was encouraged by her discovery and made up her mind to grind the flint.

The moment her bat teeth touched thallium, Sofia knew she had miscalculated its hardness. *This plan is not going to work.*

She had to come up with another solution. With precious seconds slipping by, Sofia's mind raced, trying to remember everything she had learned about bats. Then a weird realization struck her like a freight train.

Sofia looked into the firing mechanism once more. After some time, she understood that, in order for the weapon to work, the flint must strike the thallium ball first. *I need to bend or cover that thallium ball with something.*

She tried bending it, but the thing did not budge. *I must cover it then.*

She surveyed the area, thinking about what to use as a buffer, but nothing presented itself as an obvious solution. She could not risk flying around the cabin, searching for an object to lodge into the rifle. She needed something quick, but what?

Her calm composure was dissipating and changing into recklessness and panic, eyes bouncing up and down, left and right, with no real results. Then, like a rising sun on the horizon, the solution revealed itself in the form of leather upholstery on a chair situated near the rifles.

Sofia did not need to fly far before she clenched herself to the bottom of the chair. Sofia used her bat teeth to cut a leather strip from the excess of upholstery. Then she flew back. She worked on sticking one end of the leather strip on one side of the thallium ball, then extending the rest to the other side, constructing a slingshot. *When the flint hits the leather strip, it should bounce back. I hope this works.*

This process took longer than she had expected, but she was too invested at this point. There was no going back now.

As she finished up the first flint, the soldier in charge returned to the main room. The rifle Sofia stood on shook under the power of the man's walk. Sofia clenched her tiny feet to the cock of the rifle so she would not fall off it.

"This is taking too long," the soldier noted. "They were supposed to be here by now!"

The three other soldiers exchanged looks, but none offered feedback.

Sofia stood, frozen in time and space, as the soldier's words echoed in her ears. "*Our source said they should be here shortly.*"

Who is this source they are talking about? Excluding Roderick and Dalia, the only other people she could think of were Dalia's crew or Hazard.

There was no time to think more about it. She had a more important task to conclude.

While the soldiers talked about the mysterious source, Sofia jumped over to the second rifle. She climbed onto the flintlock mechanism and went to work. She flew back beneath the leather chair and cut an almost identical strip of leather.

One soldier walked over to the chair where Sofia was hiding and rested his bottom on the chair. Sofia held tightly onto the bottom of the chair as the upholstery pushed down violently under the pressure of the soldier's body. *This is both good and bad.* Good, because Sofia was concealed from the others, and bad because the soldier could easily hear her attaching the strap to the rifle. *There is no way I can finish the job unnoticed. I need to find a distraction.*

Sparks filled her bat brain, bouncing back and forth, trying to find the hole in which they could fall and push out the answer to her question, like a slot machine spitting out coins when hitting the jackpot.

Sofia released her grip from the bottom of the chair and flew behind the sitting soldier until she reached the naphtha lamp situated on the dresser near Bartholomeu. Using her mouth, she turned a dial on the side of the lamp until she fully extinguished the fire. *To bring back the light, they will need to produce the fire first. This should buy me some time.*

Darkness consumed the room, making it impossible to see a finger in front of your face. However, Sofia's new eyes were accustomed to this environment. It was captivating to watch as the soldiers stumbled around in the middle of the room, trying to escape this unforeseen situation. She knew it would take a minute or two until their eyes adapted to the darkness, so she flew swiftly to the second rifle and continued to work on the slingshot contraption.

As she continued to work on the rifle, the anxious soldiers kept moving around the room, producing a noisy cover for her secretive work. They sounded like a herd of sheep stomping around a barn, expecting to go out into the wild.

"I think I found matches," one of the soldiers spoke.

Oh no. I have to hurry.

The leather strap was almost wrapped around the side of the rifle. Her little feet worked overtime as they tried to complete the job before the light returned to the cabin.

As she prepared herself for departure, Sofia decided there was one more thing she had to do.

She flew from the rifle to the front door and landed on the metal lock. She grabbed it with her teeth and pushed it to the left, unlocking the door. She then flew back toward the fireplace right as the room lit up, revealing four confused men and Bartholomeu, all staring at the lamp, hypnotized.

I did it! Sofia exhaled, briskly flying out of the chimney and into the moonlit sky above.

Sofia did a victory lap in the air before returning to the alley across the street where Roderick patiently waited for her arrival. There was something weird about seeing herself next to Roderick from this perspective. She thought the two of them looked good next to each other. She quickly dismissed the thought as she flew to her human hand, transforming back into a paper animal.

Sofia gasped for air as her senses returned to her human body. Then she pulled the box from her pocket and placed the paper bat into it.

She turned to Roderick, grinning from ear to ear. "There are four soldiers inside, and they have Bartholomeu tied to a chair. I disabled two rifles and unlocked the front door. One of them still has a pistol at his waist, and they all carry blades."

Roderick looked at Sofia. "You did all that while inside? That's impressive," Roderick said, smiling. "I noticed the light go out and got fearful for your life. What happened?"

"Oh, you know," Sofia replied, pushing her bangs to the left to clear her forehead. "I shut the light off so I could work in darkness. That's a new thing I found out I could do. Being a bat is pretty cool."

"What?" Roderick said, shaking his head.

Sofia gave Roderick a full description of the cabin and where all the furniture, rifles, and Bartholomeu were seated.

"You did a great job," Roderick complimented her. "I now need you to stay put while I deal with the soldiers. Hopefully, the door is still unlocked because that's going to be the focal point for my surprise attack."

Roderick unsheathed his sword and took a long deep breath in. He held it for several seconds before releasing the tension through his mouth. "Please stay hidden while I finish the job," Roderick begged Sofia, who had already started to pace back and forth in the dark alleyway.

"Please be careful," Sofia exclaimed, her hands suddenly turning cold.

Roderick nodded and then ran across the street.

CHAPTER 19

Without stopping or slowing down, Roderick kicked the door inward. He immediately found himself on top of one of the enemies and pierced his gut with the sword. Seconds passed before the other two soldiers regained enough composure to throw themselves into the fight.

The second engaged Roderick in a sword fight. The third one rushed for one of the rifles.

He picked up a rifle, snuggled it tightly against his shoulder, aimed at Roderick, and pulled the trigger. A click of the hammer hitting air surprised the soldier. He looked at the rifle in utter confusion, cocked it again, and fired once more. He got the same result as before—nothing but a click.

In the meantime, Roderick blocked an overhead attack, then counterattacked by kicking his adversary in the gut with his right foot, followed by a swift slash of a sword across the chest. The second soldier looked down at the damage and collapsed to his knees. Blood gushed out of his chest.

Roderick's attention now switched to the soldier with the rifle as the soldier struggled to level the second rifle in his direction. Once he succeeded, the second rifle made the same lifeless clicking sound. By then, Roderick was within arm's length of the soldier. He stabbed him through his heart.

As Roderick turned around to look for the fourth man, his arms suddenly hugged his body, dropping the sword against his will. Roderick faced the commanding soldier, a tall, burly man who was twice as wide as Roderick. The soldier slammed Roderick into the wooden floorboards so hard that the breath was forced from his lungs. By the time he'd recovered, the large soldier was sitting on top of him.

Roderick looked death in the eyes. His death had a long, red goatee, hairless head, and pretty green eyes. Roderick's arms were still tightly bound to his body, forcefully squeezed by the soldier's knees.

Slowly, the soldier raised his hand, holding a short blade. The blade moved downward in the direction of Roderick's heart, and he could do nothing about it. Roderick closed his eyes.

His body suddenly became lighter, free.

He opened his eyes to find the soldier was not towering above him any longer. He raised his head up slightly and was greeted by something spectacular. Something he had never anticipated seeing, something so deadly yet so beautiful.

A bear stood above the soldier's lifeless body, dripping blood over his unseeing green eyes. The bear then made short eye contact with Roderick before it ran out of the cabin. Several moments later, Sofia emerged through the front door.

****

"Are you all right?" she asked, rushing to tend to Roderick's invisible wounds.

"I am now," Roderick answered.

After they regrouped from yet another fight, Roderick and Sofia approached Bartholomeu, who was still tied to a chair several feet away. Sofia untied the old man and removed the gag from his mouth.

The first thing he said was, "Please, get me some water."

Sofia looked around, stepping over two dead bodies to get to the bucket of water sitting on the dining room table. She found a ladle nearby, scooped the water with it, and spoon-fed Bartholomeu until he regained his senses.

"Who . . .? Who are you?" Bartholomeu asked, still struggling with his senses.

Roderick got down on his left knee to be at eye level with Bartholomeu. "My name is Roderick Cross, and this is Princess Elan of Thalia. Master Fry sent us here to find you."

Bartholomeu stared at Roderick, then at Sofia. "That bear from earlier, was that what I think it was?"

"Yes," Sofia answered.

"I never thought I would witness light magic in my lifetime," Bartholomeu said, looking at Sofia and admiring her posture and confidence. "Is Edgar still alive?"

"Yes, he is. He sent us to find you after we collected all sources of light magic," Sofia said.

"Oh, yes, of course," Bartholomeu said. "It was beautiful. I'd only heard and read about the light magic, but witnessing it is something undeniably satisfying. Remarkable!"

"I have a question to ask you, Bartholomeu," Sofia said as she moved closer. She looked at Roderick, then back at Bartholomeu. "How did these men know we were coming?"

Bartholomeu moved his eyes from Sofia to Roderick. "That I do not know. They showed up several hours ago, barged into my home, and tied me up. I heard them talk of someone coming, but I never guessed it could be you, Princess Elan herself."

"Interesting," Roderick said.

"We are here because Master Fry said you could show us the hidden entrance to the castle," Roderick added.

"I can help you with that, for sure. Could you first help an old man clean the house of this garbage?" Bartholomeu asked, pointing at the four dead bodies spread across the floor.

"Of course we can help you with that," Roderick said. He and Sofia removed the bodies, dropping them into the dark alleyway across the street.

After a quick cleanup, Bartholomeu told Roderick and Sofia all they needed to hear concerning the secret entrance to the castle. He even drew a map of how to get there from his house on a piece of cloth. This was not the fastest nor the shortest route, but he considered two things when making the map. One was that certain streets had a large royal guard presence. The other was the route had to go through the pub district of the lower city where they could find Dalia.

"The secret passage is located in a small private school in the lower city that closed its doors to children sixteen moons ago," Bartholomeu said. "It is abandoned, and no one should be inside. I would exercise caution, though. I have seen more royal guards in the lower city recently than ever before."

"Thank you for your help, Bartholomeu," Sofia said.

"Anything Your Highness desires," Bartholomeu said. "However, I have a suggestion for you," he added.

"Please, say it," Sofia said.

"I suggest you separate some of the sources of magic in case something goes wrong. You do not want the queen to get ahold of everything at once."

"That's a great suggestion," Roderick interjected himself.

"I agree," Sofia replied, nodding.

Sofia pulled out the Knife of Life together with a leather satchel containing the magic paper and blueprint and handed them over to Bartholomeu.

Bartholomeu almost collapsed from excitement. He stared at the sacred items resting in his weathered hands. "It's magical," he gasped. "I . . . I do not know if I can keep these safe. You saw what happened to me with those soldiers. Who says that more will not return?"

"You are right," Sofia said. "We don't know, but none of them would suspect you would have these. That's why I think this is the safest place for them."

Bartholomeu nodded as he brought the items close to his heart. "I will keep them safe for you, Your Highness." He bowed as far as his old body would allow him.

Sofia helped him stand straight again. "No need for that, Bartholomeu. I'm not in this for the crown. I just want to help the people of Thalia get rid of the queen. Once that's done, I will return where I belong—my home."

"But this is your home," Bartholomeu said.

"It feels that way at the moment, I have to confess," Sofia responded. "As much as I like it here, I still have other things I need to take care of. It's hard to explain, and we don't have enough time for my long stories. Thank you for believing in me, and I hope that I can live up to those expectations."

Creases formed between Bartholomeu's white eyebrows. But he shook his head and changed the subject. "I almost forgot.

There is one other important thing I need to share with you." Bartholomeu waved Roderick and Sofia to follow him into his bedroom.

"I have something special for you, young man." Bartholomeu went down on his knees, removing one of the floorboards from where he pulled out a cloth bundle. Bartholomeu unwrapped the fabric on his bed, revealing six arrowheads with a baby blue tint on their sharp edges.

"Thallium!" Roderick exclaimed.

"Yes," Bartholomeu said. "I made these for this special occasion. I know there are only six of them. That was all the thallium I managed to get ahold of. I hope they will be useful against the queen's magic." Bartholomeu rewrapped the arrowheads and then handed them to Roderick. He then placed the Knife of Life and the blueprint into the same hole under his bed.

Sofia hugged him tightly as if she had known him her entire life. Then she and Roderick stepped out into the night. With hoods covering their heads and darkness covering their faces, they moved around the town, following Bartholomeu's hand-drawn map.

****

Sofia and Roderick wandered the streets of the lower city, staying close to the buildings to draw less attention. They found themselves surrounded by a plethora of pubs and adult-only establishments. The smell of karish was overwhelming. Sofia could not tell if her sense of smell had increased since she'd turned into a bat or if it was the potency of the karish itself. She felt more jumpy than usual because they had already passed by six posters featuring their faces, accompanied by the words *WANTED, DEAD OR ALIVE*.

Seeing their faces on a wanted poster, Sofia oddly felt good about it.

"We kind of look good on these posters," Sofia said, smiling as they walked past another one. Roderick looked at Sofia from the corner of his eye as he continued walking.

"Not sure if I agree with you on that," Roderick said. "But what it does show, at least for me, is the rebellion against the crown." He took a deep breath. "I wish my father was here to see it."

Roderick squeezed his collapsible bow, which he had inherited from his father, who had inherited it from Roderick's grandfather. Generations of elite soldiers were contained in that bow that now rested in Roderick's hands. Generations of pride, of sacrifice, of loyalty.

"I'm sorry for bringing up this topic," Sofia said, lowering her gaze to the ground in front of her.

"Please don't be," Roderick interjected. "It has nothing to do with you. It's hard to explain, but many things bring back the memory of my father."

"Would you like to talk about it?" Sofia asked, turning toward Roderick.

"Maybe some other time," Roderick replied. "We need to find Dalia before she gets wasted."

"She can't be too far," Sofia said. "Do you want to separate so we can cover more ground?"

"I would rather not," Roderick answered instantly. "You know how I feel about separating from you."

"Fair enough," Sofia said, her face turning bright red.

They continued looking through the windows and doors of several pubs, but there was no sign of Dalia. They crossed the street to check another fine establishment, almost identical to seven others they had already walked by. The only difference was that this pub had live music. Above the entrance was a wooden sign reading *The Pirate's Den.*

"That sounds kind of fitting," Roderick murmured. "Want to check it out?"

"We should leave no rocks unturned," Sofia said, stepping onto the decaying sidewalk and moving toward the pub. "With a name like that, I'm almost certain we'll find Dalia inside."

Hiding behind a mountain of trash that piled up by the entrance, Sofia and Roderick searched the interior of the pub until they spotted Dalia downing shots of karish in rapid succession.

"There she is," Roderick proclaimed, shaking his head.

Sofia could not shake off her disappointment as Dalia downed drinks, one after another. She looked different . . . kind of absent.

Roderick and Sofia exchanged looks.

"We need to get her out before she gets wasted to the point of no return," Sofia suggested.

"How do you intend to do that? Turn into an animal and walk into a bar full of pirates, expecting nothing but glances?" Roderick joked.

Sofia was stunned by his sarcasm, but she found it funny. "No, silly. We are going to walk in together and get her out of there."

Roderick chuckled at Sofia's suggestion. "No, seriously. How do you intend on getting her out of there?"

"I already told you," Sofia said, her eyebrows stretching to the middle of her forehead. "We are walking in there and getting her out."

"What a great idea!" Roderick replied. "Two wanted people walking into a pub full of money-thirsty pirates. What could possibly go wrong?"

Sofia smiled but offered no other explanation. She simply readjusted her hood, which now fell below her eyes, hiding them from the view of the curious. Without waiting for Roderick's approval, she barged into the pub, leaving Roderick several feet behind.

He quickly put his hood over his head and picked up the pace to catch up to Sofia in the middle of the pub. "Thanks for the heads-up," Roderick said, shaking his head at Sofia.

"Welcome," Sofia replied with a small grin on her face, clearly savoring the moment.

There was one empty chair to the right of Dalia, so Sofia slid into it. Roderick went to the other side of her and stood by, staring at the bar in front of him. The smell of liquor was overwhelming.

The bartender brought another shot of karish and placed it in front of Dalia. Before she could get ahold of the glass, though, Sofia snatched it from her.

Surprisingly swift for her current inebriated state, Dalia pulled out a short blade from her waist and placed it against Sofia's throat. "I wouldn't do that if I were you," she warned.

At that moment, the tip of a blade pushed into the side of Dalia's chest. "You drop that knife, or I will rip you like the sail of a ship in the middle of a hunting storm," Roderick whispered into Dalia's ear.

A grimace developed on Dalia's face. She turned toward Roderick, returning the knife back to her waist and ignoring Sofia for the moment. "You . . . You are alive?" she asked as she snatched the glass of karish from Sofia's hand and then downed it like a champ.

"Why wouldn't we be?" Sofia asked.

"Let's have a conversation outside the pub," Roderick suggested as he noticed various men of questionable ethics staring at them.

"We need to move, and you clearly had too much to drink," Sofia added.

Dalia turned to face Sofia, teeth showing between her trembling lips.

"Hey." Sofia shook her by the shoulder. "We got the map to the secret passage. We need to get going. Time is ticking."

Dalia shook her head, clearing her blurred vision. "Yes, of course. The secret passage. I . . . I need to use the bathroom first."

"Are you serious? You need to use the bathroom?" Roderick asked.

"Well, a girl's got to do what a girl's got to do," Dalia said, sending a grin Roderick's way.

Roderick met Sofia's eyes and then nodded toward Dalia. "Why don't you do your bathroom thing, and we'll wait for you outside?" Roderick grabbed Sofia by the arm and led her out of the pub.

CHAPTER 20

Sofia, Roderick, and Dalia moved like shadows through the alleys and streets of the capital, heading in the direction of the schoolhouse. Bartholomeu's handmade map came in handy since every street in the lower city looked identical.

Dalia's behavior had been odd ever since their arrival to the capital. Dalia did not look or act like her normal self. Sofia knew Dalia could handle karish, but this was different . . . as if she had given in to her vice and was not in control of herself.

As they walked toward their intended destination, things became even stranger. Sofia listened from the sideline to how Roderick and Dalia kept exchanging superlatives like there was no tomorrow. It felt odd seeing them laugh and agree on so many things.

Sofia's chest felt heavy. Odd discomfort lingered inside her like a rainy cloud in the absence of wind. Then, as if they had heard Sofia's frustration, Dalia and Roderick stopped talking, and silence ruled the air.

Sofia tried to ignore her two companions by preoccupying herself with thoughts of what might happen when she finally met the queen.

She knew she was not ready for this face-to-face meeting, but with everything going so fast, Sofia felt strongly that she should capitalize on her good luck.

Sofia's thoughts were interrupted by Roderick's warning to stay quiet.

Roderick looked down at Bartholomeu's map in his left hand and pressed his right index finger against his moist lips. "I think we are getting close," he whispered. "Behind that corner ahead of us." Roderick stepped in front of Sofia, who had led their party of three since they had picked up Dalia, and rested his back flat against the wall of a nearby house. He peeked around the corner and then retreated at once.

"Great," he said, not looking surprised at all. "There are two guards in front of the house."

"Do you think they knew we were coming?" Sofia asked as she peeked around the corner to see what Roderick had seen. "Why would they guard this place unless they knew what lay on the other side of it or that we were coming?"

"If they knew about it, they would wait for us inside and not make it so obvious. I think they just happened to be standing there, being lazy," Roderick offered.

"Makes sense," Sofia replied.

"What do you think we should do?"

Roderick pulled out the collapsible bow from his belt and held it in front of him.

"I wouldn't do that," Dalia spoke up. "I think we should use a distraction to deal with them."

"What kind of distraction?" Roderick inquired.

Dalia looked over at Sofia.

“You mean me?” Sofia asked with a heavy feeling in her stomach.

“Yes, you, or one of your animal creatures, or whatever you call them,” Dalia suggested. “Personally, I would love to see what you are made of, little princess, but I’ll be satisfied even if you use that magic of yours.” Dalia rolled her eyes.

Sofia did not want to overthink what Dalia really meant with that statement.

Sofia pulled her origami box from the inside of her tunic and ran her gentle fingers over the paper creatures resting inside. After a short debate between the bat and the mouse, she chose the mouse.

Sofia gently lifted the paper mouse out of the box and placed it into the palm of her right hand. She used the other hand to return the box to her tunic.

No words were exchanged between the three of them as Sofia flicked the paper mouse into the air, and a little brown mouse landed on the cobblestone street in front of Dalia and Roderick. At the same time, Sofia’s body stood next to them in eerie silence.

Without hesitation, Sofia the mouse tiptoed in the direction of the guards.

As the mouse approached the guards, Dalia pulled out a blade from her waist while Roderick pulled out a single arrow.

Sofia quickly closed the gap between her and the guards.

What am I doing? She had never talked to Roderick and Dalia about what her distraction was going to be, and she did not even have one in mind. Not at the moment, anyway.

Looking left then right while crossing the street, Sofia approached the guard closest to her and stopped short of biting his leg. *Biting might be too extreme*. Sofia was afraid the guard would scream in pain, which would then draw unnecessary attention. Sofia filled her mouse heart with courage and climbed on top of the guard's boot. At first, she chewed on his laces to get his attention, but it seemed this was not doing the trick. Sofia then moved higher up the boot and scratched the guard's sock.

The guard looked down. When he spotted a mouse hanging on to his leg, he kicked his foot high and gasped in horror, hoping to send the vermin flying. Sofia kept her composure and held on to the guard's boot.

"What the hell?" the guard yelled, kicking at his vermin-infested leg with the other leg.

The other guard watched in amusement as his partner fought a war with a tiny, cute mouse before he broke into laughter. "There is nothing better than to watch a grown man scream like a little girl," the guard said, laughing as he placed both hands on his stomach.

By now, both guards were facing away from Dalia and Roderick, clearly preoccupied with the unusual scene. This gave Dalia and Roderick enough time to approach the guards from the rear. They returned their weapons to their belts and moved in. They picked their targets, then subdued them with barely any effort. As Dalia and Roderick pulled the bodies into a nearby alley, the little mouse ran back to where Sofia's body stood and climbed up her leg until it reached the hand holding the bracelet. In a moment, Sofia regained consciousness, finding the paper critter in her palm. Sofia looked at the paper mouse and could swear she saw it smile.

Moments later, all three met in front of the house.

"That was reckless!" Roderick addressed Sofia in a stern voice. "Next time, you should share your plan with me so at least I know what to expect."

Sofia smiled at Roderick's words but said nothing. She knew he was right and that he was voicing his concern.

Roderick moved to the front door and grabbed the doorknob. He found it locked.

Before he could say anything, Dalia forced her way between him and Sofia. She pulled out a lock-picking kit from one of her pockets and took two things out of the tiny tin box. She inserted a wire into the lock, followed by a thicker metal piece. She gently swayed the wire from left to right until a click was heard.

"You did it!" Sofia hopped as she spoke.

Dalia frowned at Sofia. "I wouldn't celebrate yet, if I were you, little princess." Dalia pushed the wooden door. The door opened in conjunction with a squeaking sound produced by its rusty hinges. "Let's go."

****

It was pitch dark and humid inside the structure. Roderick reached into his pocket and then pulled out a dynamo flashlight, which she squeezed several times, causing the motor to hum and produce enough energy to illuminate the entire room.

The house was one big open room with no other doors in sight. The room was filled with bookcases, displaying a variety of books from history to literature to science. It was an impressive collection.

Books? I thought all paper was banned and destroyed? How could this be right here under the queen's nose? Sofia continued surveying the room.

There was a cube-like pedestal positioned in the center of the room, with no chairs in sight. It looked like an enclosed box with no doors or drawers. An old-looking balance scale was sitting on top of it with a single weight resting in one of its trays. All three separated to look at and touch the books stacked on the shelves in front of them.

Sofia pulled down a book titled *History of Thalia Through the Centuries*. She opened the book and was greeted by pages made out of fabric. *This is not paper*. She then pulled another book, *Ancient Architecture*, and another, *Culture of the Thalian Kingdom*. With each book, she found the same results between their bindings—pages made out of fabric.

Minutes into their research of the books, the dynamo motor of the flashlight made a concerning dying sound, only to be awakened seconds later by another set of quick squeezes.

"What are we looking for?" Roderick asked, looking at the books in front of him.

Dalia turned around to face Roderick. "There has to be a way to get to the castle from here. There must be a secret passage in this room."

Sofia knew Dalia was right; she needed to find the answer to this riddle that was hidden within these four walls.

Roderick was already on the floor, testing the wooden planks for different sounds. Dalia kept removing books, one by one, looking for a secret unlocking mechanism. Sofia knelt on the floor in front of her bookcase, looking for anything that might be worth manipulating. As she searched for clues, a cool breeze hit the front of her neck.

"Did you guys feel that breeze?" Sofia asked.

Roderick and Dalia looked at her with puzzled expressions.

"Breeze?" Dalia asked. "No, I didn't feel any breeze."

"I swear I felt something," Sofia continued. "It felt nice and soothing as if someone blew cold air onto my neck." Sofia opened her origami box and pulled out one paper animal randomly. It happened to be a bear. She placed the paper bear on the floor in front of the bookcase. The paper glided over the surface of the floor toward the middle of the room.

Sofia picked up the paper bear and placed it on the floor in front of Roderick's bookcase. The bear did not move at all. As Sofia went around the room, testing other bookcases, none of them performed as the one that she had tried first, so Sofia returned the bear to the first bookcase. The paper bear once more glided across the floor.

"Gods, you are up to something!" Roderick said.

"There must be something behind that bookcase."

As they gathered in front of the bookcase in question, Roderick brought his flashlight to life once again. They removed the books, then tried to push and pull on the empty bookcase. Nothing worked. The bookcase appeared to be an integral part of the wall. Trying to break the bookcase would cause too much noise, so that option was out of the question.

"There must be something simple. It's always that way. You do everything you imagine you can do, and at the very end, it ends up being something so stupidly simple," Roderick professed as he picked up one book from the floor and examined it.

"What if the bookcase can only be opened from the other side?" Sofia asked.

"That's an interesting theory," Dalia joined the conversation. "How about you transform into that rat thing and start munching on the wood?"

Sofia looked at Dalia, sensing sarcasm in her voice. She hated to admit it, but there was some validity to her suggestion. However, she was not ready to transform into one of her magical creatures to test Dalia's theory. It would take her hours to eat through the bookcase to make a large enough hole in it so that she could get through.

Daylight was not too far away, and the two guards outside would soon be discovered. Or they might wake up on their own and alarm others. They needed to figure this out quickly.

Sofia turned her head to the center of the room. *How ignorant of me. I concentrated on the bookcases while this thing stood in the middle of the room, begging for attention.*

"What about this scale thing?" she suggested, intrigued by its randomness in a room full of books. "Don't you think it's a little odd for a scale to be here with all these books? It looks like something needs to be placed into the other pan to find the perfect balance."

Dalia and Roderick looked at each other.

"Is this your intuition talking?" Roderick inquired.

"Kind of, I guess. It just feels right," she answered, unsure of her answer.

She picked up a random book from the ground and placed it on an empty tray, but the scale did not move a bit. She then placed another one. *Still nothing.* As she placed the third book on the scale, slow movement of the scale got their attention, followed by a rattling noise from behind the bookcase.

"Did you hear that?" Roderick exclaimed. "Something moved behind that bookcase. Keep going. You are doing great," he encouraged.

Sofia placed another book, which then brought the trays closer to a perfect balance. The rattling noise behind the bookcase returned, but nothing more than that happened.

Another book placed on the scale tipped the balance in favor of the books. The bookcase stood its ground and did not open.

"I think you are close. You need to find the right books for that perfect balance," Dalia offered.

Find the right books. There was something interesting about Dalia's statement. Sofia sensed she was on the right path, but things were more complicated than they looked. There were hundreds of books in the room.

Sofia shifted her energy into a higher gear and kept placing and removing books from the scale. She was greeted with the same result—failure. She always went above the weight, tipping the scale in favor of the books, but could never find that perfect balance. She shifted books again, compared their thickness, evaluated their sizes, but none of it worked.

Thirty minutes passed. They all started to lose hope that they would pick the right combination. Then, during another attempt, the scale made a different rattling sound. Six books stood on one side of the scale, in perfect balance with the other side, and the rattling noise turned into grinding. The bookcase stayed put.

"What now?" Roderick asked.

"I don't know," Sofia responded. "It seems we balanced the scale perfectly. I don't know why it's not opening."

As Sofia circled the table, looking for other clues, her eyes connected with the books on the scale. *What are you hiding from me?* She glazed over the titles, and an anagram formed before her eyes. Looking at the first letters of each title, *LAITHA* stared back at her.

Laitha? Athila . . . Thaila! Oh my God! It's Thalia!

Sofia jumped toward the scale, lifting the books and rearranging them in a different order as Dalia and Roderick stood fast, watching her.

The top book started with the letter *T,* and the bottom book with the letter *A*. The moment she finished her rearrangement and the titles of the books spelled THALIA, a loud clicking sound came from the direction of the bookcase. The bookcase shook, forming a small cloud of dust in front of it as it moved into the wall. Moments later, a dark gap stood in the place where the bookcase had once stood.

Sofia stared at the hole, mesmerized. She was happy that she had managed to solve the puzzle but also worried about what was waiting for her on the other side. She was much closer to meeting the queen than ever before.

Dalia, Roderick, and Sofia walked closer to the wall. Two steps later, all three were consumed by the darkness that lay beyond.

CHAPTER 21

Roderick grabbed the handle of his sword as he dug his feet into the ground. When nothing came out of the dark void, they ventured into the tunnel's depths.

The tunnel was pitch black, but thanks to the dynamo flashlight, the darkness came to life, revealing years of simple but precise craftsmanship. The walls appeared to be made of the same material as the rest of the castle, indicating the passage was built at the same time.

They strolled forward for some time until they started moving in a downward angle, cutting deeper into the mountain the castle rested on.

Roderick brought the flashlight to life two more times before they reached something other than the bare rocks of the tunnel—a metal gate blocking their only path into the castle.

"Yet another obstacle," Sofia said in frustration.

"I bet Dalia can unlock this one with ease," Roderick added.

Dalia approached the gate, grabbing the metal doorknob. The door swung open without protest. "There you go," she said as she walked straight through it.

Sofia and Roderick exchanged looks, shrugged, and then followed Dalia through the gate.

The tunnel exuded a slight eeriness as if telling them to turn around and run while they still could.

Sofia ignored the cries of cowardice as she pushed forward. *What could possibly go wrong?* She had survived many things against all odds, and that was before she had the power of magic on her side.

As they traveled deeper into the tunnel, the air became more humid. Roderick's flashlight hummed to a stop, and they found themselves in total darkness once more. When he tried to bring it back to life, the flashlight refused to cooperate.

"It's not working," Roderick exclaimed in frustration.

"Let's not panic," Dalia said. "We need to stay up against the wall and follow it forward. Eventually, it will lead us to the end."

"I think I should transform into a bat to check what lays before us," Sofia spoke up. "As a bat, I can see better in the darkness."

Dalia and Roderick did not disagree with Sofia's assessment, but before they could verbally agree, Sofia was already reaching for her box and feeling for the paper bat.

"I'll be right back," she said as she released the paper bat from her right palm.

Sofia fluttered in the tunnel for a short time before she disappeared into the darkness.

As she flew through the tunnel, she came to an intersection with two paths. Sofia turned left. This was the first time she smelled a strong odor of feces in the tunnel. In an instant, she knew she was in the sewer.

She did not know if this was because bats had a better sense of smell than humans or because the smell did not reach as far as where she had left her human self.

A short distance ahead of her, a dim light shone from above, forming a cone-like shape as it hit the bottom of the tunnel.

As Sofia approached the light source, she saw an opening at the top of the tunnel revealing the full moon glowing in the dark sky above. There was a metal grate over the opening to allow rainwater to come through. It was secured by two latches that appeared to be rusted, indicating no one had used them recently.

Sofia spun around to look in the other direction. It appeared the tunnel continued straight ahead, so she continued flying further until she reached another light source about fifty feet ahead of her. This light, however, was less intense than the one before. When she reached it and looked up, she was greeted by another grate, but no moon in sight.

Sofia landed on the metal cover and pushed herself out of it. She stood on the cover for a short time, taking in the sights around her. She was standing in the courtyard of the castle where a couple of soldiers stood on top of a watchtower on the opposite side.

She flew up into the air to get a full aerial view of the area. The first thing that caught her attention was the cover that she had come out of was much better concealed than the first one. It was shaded by a concrete post. Sofia also noticed a number of soldiers in the tower. A large wooden gate crisscrossed by metal rods separated the courtyard from the rest of the castle. The only way to the other side would be via the front gate.

Sofia flew to the other side of the wooden gate, where she found two soldiers standing guard. *This is not going to be easy, but it could've been much worse. I need to check if the tunnel continues further into the castle.*

She continued flying until she reached another gate, but this one was open. There was a drawbridge ahead of it and darkness below. Sofia could not see what lay beneath the bridge, despite the moonlight.

On the other side of the drawbridge was a series of barracks, most likely housing the royal guard. *Our only way in would be through the main gate. I just need to figure out how to get in.*

When Sofia returned to the sewer tunnel, she turned right, in the direction of the castle. She continued flying for another fifty feet until she reached the end of the tunnel. There was a small hole at the bottom of the wall from where sewage water continuously flowed. *Hmm, there is something odd about this.* Sofia inspected the wall in front of her. *Edgar never mentioned we had to exit the tunnel.*

As she internally debated, other smells reached Sofia's nostrils. *It smells like . . . like fresh cement.* She scanned the wall, spotting evidence of recent construction. *Something was done here recently. But why? Why would they put a wall down here? To stop us from entering? That would mean they know we are coming. What happened at Bartholomeu's house can't be a coincidence. I don't like any of this.*

Sofia left the cement wall and flew back to her body, opening her eyes to feel the paper bat resting in her right palm. She shook her head for a moment as she placed the bat back into the box, then explained to Roderick and Dalia what she had seen. The three of them briefly discussed the situation before they continued their stroll, heading toward the cement wall.

As they faced the wall, they inspected it more thoroughly. They agreed on one thing—the wall had recently been constructed—but they couldn't agree on which way to go from that point. Sofia and Roderick voted for the option involving the metal cover as their way into the castle. Dalia suggested they should exploit the newly constructed wall as their primary entry point. Two votes for the metal cover prevailed, and the trio moved toward the metal cover despite Dalia's protest.

They inspected the hinges from a crouched position. Then Dalia pulled out one of her knives and scraped at the rust that had accumulated on the hinges. She almost cut herself several times due to the poor lighting and also had to stop several times as soldiers walked right above them, conducting their rounds. The scraping of the rust was more intense and time-consuming than any of them had expected.

About thirty minutes later, Dalia had removed enough rust to open the metal cover. Roderick tried pushing it upward, but it refused to give. After several more minutes of scraping the rust, the cover finally moved, but not enough for a full-sized human to pass through.

"I have an idea," Sofia said, reaching for her trusted animal box. "I could use my mouse teeth to scrape off the rest of the rust. I just need one of you to lift me and hold me there so I can work on it. It's going to be much easier that way."

"I'll do it," Roderick offered without hesitation.

After another transformation, Roderick held Sofia in her mouse form up against the metal cover as she pressed her front teeth against the rusted hinges. She worked tirelessly, almost to the point of enjoying herself.

In about five minutes, Sofia finished one hinge and moved to another, which took half the time as the first. Then she turned her head toward Roderick, who placed the mouse in Sofia's right palm, and the flesh of a live mouse transformed back into its paper form.

"I think it's ready," Sofia said, satisfied with her work.

Roderick carefully pushed the cover upward and did not find any resistance. He held the cover with his right hand, suspended in the air, while pushing himself off the ground and through the opening. Sofia followed in the same manner.

When she was out, Dalia handed over her blades to Roderick. She mimicked their movement until she was crouched next to them behind the sole concrete post in the outer courtyard as the royal guard paraded above them. Dalia then grabbed her blades from Roderick.

"Now what?" Dalia asked.

Sofia glanced at her.

"I have an idea," Sofia whispered. "I'll change into a fox and sneak up to the other side of the gate. I'll go through the watchtower on the opposite side of the courtyard."

"And then what?" Roderick asked.

"I'll try to unlock the gate from the other side to give us easier access to the rest of the castle."

"But we still need to deal with the two soldiers on the other side of the gate," Roderick pointed out.

"True," Sofia agreed. "With the element of surprise, if everything goes smoothly, we should be able to get past them. That sounds easier than dealing with the soldiers above us."

"I trust your decision," Roderick said, looking straight into Sofia's eyes.

With the discussion over, Sofia found herself in the shape of a fox. She moved silently against the castle wall, heading toward the stairs leading up to the watchtower on the other side of the courtyard. She looked left then right before she proceeded up the stairs. When she reached the landing, a strong stench from one of the soldiers attacked her nostrils.

Sofia moved into a shadow inside the guard tower closest to her, waiting for the soldier to walk by. It was a close call, as the soldier almost stepped on Sofia's tail. She had the position of the moon and her small body to thank for not being spotted.

Once the soldier went by, Sofia ran in the direction of the second watchtower. If her calculations were correct, no soldiers should be there.

She moved gracefully over the cold stone pathway until she reached the second tower, exercising due diligence, despite the fact that she could not see or smell any humans around. Sofia moved through the tower until she was on the other side of the wall, then stopped next to the stairs identical to those that she had used to climb up. These, however, led down to the other side of the large gate, where two soldiers stood guard. One was resting on his rifle near the gate, while the other one was leaning against the gate itself.

Sofia crept down. When she reached the bottom of the stairs, she slipped to the right, keeping close to the wall, protected by the darkness of the night. She moved toward the main courtyard, which opened up to a vast space housing multiple barracks, most likely used for military purposes.

Sofia surveyed the immediate area and did not notice anyone else around. *This is perfect.* Sofia ran across the courtyard to the other side, where she found several buckets used for carrying water.

Sofia approached one of the metal buckets resting on top of a wooden table and pushed it over, producing enough noise to reach the two soldiers at the gate.

"Who's there?" one of them yelled, startled by the noise.

The two soldiers readied their rifles as they walked toward the source of the noise.

Sofia hurriedly stepped through the spilled water, leaving her paw prints for the soldiers to find. She then retreated into the darkness of the shadowed wall behind her.

"Identify yourself!" one soldier warned as they both continued walking toward Sofia's location.

Sofia crept against the wall, still concealed by the darkness of the night. She passed the soldiers going in the opposite direction. Within seconds, she was at the gate, looking for the locking mechanism. A large wooden post was sitting in the middle of the gate. To unlock it, she would have to be more than a fox. *I'll have to turn into a dragon if I want to get through this door. It's no surprise they have two soldiers guarding this post.*

Realizing her plan had faltered, Sofia ran back up the same stairs that she had come from and disappeared into the watchtower. At the same moment, two soldiers on the other side of the gate returned to their posts, laughing.

****

Reunited with her companions, Sofia explained the current situation to them.

Roderick looked at both Dalia and Sofia, clenching his fists. "There must be another way in," he said. "Maybe we can risk it and get up on the tower the way you did?"

Dalia frowned at the idea. “I think that’s too risky. Our only way in is through the wall in the sewer.” She pointed in the direction of the tunnel’s new addition. “I think it wouldn’t be a bad idea to see what’s behind it,” Dalia said convincingly.

“Are you saying—”

“Yes,” Dalia cut off Sofia’s question. “I think you should transform back into the mouse thingy and go through the little opening in the wall to see what lies beyond. You might find something on the other side that could help us get in.”

Roderick looked at Dalia and then at Sofia. “Please tell me you are not seriously considering this as an option? It’s too risky. Someone was in the tunnels recently, building that wall.”

Sofia considered both suggestions for a moment. “I don’t know what I think anymore,” she professed. “I’m not saying this is the smartest thing to do, but I think there is some validity to Dalia’s suggestion. Considering that our other option is to face soldiers with rifles and bows, I think I must at least consider it.” Sofia looked at Dalia, who quickly broke eye contact.

Neither Roderick nor Dalia offered another suggestion. Sofia pulled out the paper mouse from the box once more and placed it in her right palm. “Are you going to wait for me here, or are you coming down with me?”

“I think we should wait here,” Dalia suggested. “You should be able to easily climb up and down the wall and through the metal cover,” Dalia elaborated.

Roderick agreed by nodding his head.

Sofia looked at Roderick and Dalia, searching for signs of regret, but she found none. The only thing she could find was Roderick’s concerned face and Dalia’s total detachment.

As a mouse, Sofia ran until she reached the little opening in the wall. The sewer smelled okay in her rodent form. She entered the hole, which was some ten feet in length. *This is too thick of a wall to bring down without being heard by the soldiers above,* Sofia considered.

As she lumbered forward, she could not get Dalia's face out of her head. *That look on her face . . .* Sofia's thought trailed off. *What was it about her face? She hasn't looked like herself since we arrived in the capital, drinking like a pirate, looking surprised to see us at the pub, hesitant and apprehensive about things.*

As Sofia reached the end of the short tunnel carved into the wall, a cold sensation rushed through her rodent body. It was as if someone had dumped a bucket of ice water over her. It woke Sofia's senses up and brought Dalia back to her thoughts. *I know that face—the face of deceit.*

Sofia tried to comprehend what she was considering when her small feet felt a different texture beneath them as she exited the tunnel. It felt unnatural.

As she took several steps forward, a loud snapping noise filled the space around her. An invisible door came down from nowhere, closing the entrance to the small tunnel behind her. Sofia panicked and tried to run forward, just to find her face slamming into an invisible wall. She could not smell anything anymore. All smells had evaporated in an instant.

Sofia looked around when the floor beneath her shook violently, sending her into another invisible wall to her immediate left. She found herself floating in the air. However, she was not floating; she was being carried away.

A royal soldier held Sofia inside a glass enclosure, trapped like the mouse she was, and now she finally understood the meaning of all this.

Dalia's face was not the face of deceit; it was the face of treason. Everything made sense now, starting with the drinking, the surprise on her face at seeing them alive, the royal guard at Bartholomeu's house, and Dalia's suggestion that she should go through the hole in the wall. Dalia had clearly led her into a trap. Dalia, the girl in black, the girl she had almost considered a friend. The same girl who had stabbed her in the back and sold her to the queen. All along, Dalia had pretended to care . . . pretended to be on her side.

****

"What's taking her so long?" Roderick asked, fidgeting with the sword in his hands.

"She'll be here any moment," Dalia tried to reassure him.

"How can you be so confident about that? You know I hate being separated from her."

"I get it," Dalia said, shifting her gaze to the ground in front of her feet. "She always returned alive from all other situations, didn't she?" Dalia reiterated. "You need to be patient, and it will all be all right."

"She did return alive, but I also happened to be at the right place at the right time to pull her out of trouble. Who says that this time will not be one of those scenarios when she actually needs my help?"

"I think you should worry less." Dalia used her compassionate voice.

Moments later, the sound of the gate opening broke the silence.

"Get down," Roderick whispered to Dalia as he ducked behind the concrete pole.

Dalia moved behind him as the courtyard filled up with twenty royal guards who positioned themselves around their hiding spot with their weapons at the ready.

"Can they see us?" Roderick asked.

He received no answer.

One man, clearly in charge of the others, walked through the gate behind the soldiers' platoon.

The man pulled his sword out and spoke. "Roderick Cross, drop your weapon and surrender yourself."

"How do they know?" Roderick whispered.

He readied his blade when something cold scratched against his throat.

"I wouldn't do that if I were you."

He looked down and recognized the familiar blade resting against his Adam's apple. Dalia's blade.

"What are you doing? Are you out of your mind?" Roderick demanded.

"Don't make this any harder than it has to be. Get up slowly, and if you try anything, I will slit your throat before you make another sound."

Roderick stood.

"Move," Dalia commanded.

Roderick moved out of the shadow of the concrete barrier with Dalia right behind him. Soon, he found himself on his knees before the chief guard, stripped of his weapons. The chief guard commanded his men to shackle Roderick and take Sofia's body, which still stood motionless in the shadows.

"How could you!" Roderick yelled, looking at Dalia, who refused to look him in the eyes.

"I trusted you."

Roderick closed his eyes as his muscles resisted being strapped and shackled.

"The first thing I will do when I get out of these shackles," Roderick said, "is to find you and kill you."

****

Hours after the first sighting of Sofia in Tarin, Dalia Swiftblade had been at the capital, preparing the *Sky Serpent* for another voyage to a faraway land, a voyage in search of people wanted by the royal court for their disobedience to the crown. Whatever they had done, it mattered not to Dalia because she was getting paid pretty well for her services.

That morning at the capital, four royal guardsmen had approached Dalia at the docks.

"Captain Swiftblade!" barked the man.

"Who wants to know?" Dalia responded, unnerved by the threatening appearance of the guard.

"Commander Trax of the royal guard. You must come with us to the castle. The queen requests your appearance."

Dalia stood there in shock for a moment. She had never met the queen, and she had never thought the queen would even know who she was. Why would she?

"W-What?" Dalia stuttered.

"Your appearance is requested by the queen. You need to come with us at once."

The ride in the royal carriage was unpleasant. Not because the wooden seating was uncomfortable but because of Commander Trax's glare.

Dalia turned her head away from Trax's piercing eyes, pretending she did not mind his scrutiny.

Commander Trax was in charge of the castle's defenses. He was also the queen's military adviser and someone who would soon reach the top of the military hierarchy.

Through the small window of the royal carriage, the richly decorated front gate of the castle appeared.

Dalia was led through the royal castle's corridors, ornamented by the royal seal of Thalia and maps of the kingdom, detailing names of all the cities and towns in its grip.

They finally reached a large, mahogany door covered with the golden dragons of the queen's crest.

Commander Trax pushed forward as the large door opened on its own accord, revealing royal soldiers on either side of a red walkway stretching from the doorway to the throne where the queen sat.

Hundreds of moons had gone into building this palace. It had taken just as many moons to decorate it from the inside out. So much history was tied to this hall. Many kings and queens had walked its marble floors, and now Dalia was walking beside them.

As they reached the end of the red carpet covering the beautiful gray marble floor, Commander Trax went down on his left knee and bowed to the queen. The other four soldiers flanking Dalia mimicked the commander's actions, leaving her alone in a standing position, caught off guard. She tried to kneel but was interrupted by her majesty, Queen Prima.

"It is all right, my dear," the queen spoke as she snapped her fingers, making the four soldiers and their commander move out of her way silently and quickly. "You probably asked yourself why I requested your appearance, my dear."

Dalia nodded and coughed at the same time to clear her throat before she spoke any words. “Yes, Your Majesty. I can’t say I wasn’t surprised. Such an invitation can’t be refused.”

“Well said, my dear.” The queen grinned. “As you suspect by now, I know a lot about you, Captain Dalia Swiftblade.”

Dalia’s heart almost stopped beating.

“I heard your skills in locating and capturing the scum that roams my kingdom is unmatched.”

A breath of relief rushed out of Dalia’s mouth. “I don’t know who said such a thing, but I don’t plan to argue that statement, Your Majesty.”

The queen released a fullhearted laugh. She approached Dalia on the podium below the throne. “Smart, beautiful, and ruthless. You remind me of my early days,” the queen said, circling Dalia. “I requested your appearance because I have a job offer for you.”

“I’m all ears, Your Majesty,” Dalia said.

“I need you to fly to Tarin and find my little sister. She was seen in town a night ago. She escaped capture . . . for now. The royal court will issue a warrant for her death or capture as a ruse to give you time to befriend her. I cannot show to my inferiors that I have a soft spot. If someone else captures her, there is a possibility they will execute her. I need you to keep her alive, and if someone gets in your way—and some will do whatever is necessary to capture her for themselves—I want you to help her escape them and help her obtain all sources of light magic, then bring her back to me. Before you do so, you must earn her trust.

“Bring her to me with all of the magic sources, and you will be rewarded handsomely. Commander Trax will give you a communication device through which you will contact him directly with any updates,” Queen Prima said. She handed Dalia a single piece of cloth with Sofia's face painted on it. "Find her and bring her alive."

CHAPTER 22

Trapped in the body of a mouse, inside a glass box, Sofia struggled not to dwell on the jail cell in Tarin and the execution she barely escaped. The only difference this time was that she had less chance of getting out. If she had been in her mouse body in Tarin, she would not have had a problem getting out; that was for sure.

The feeling that someone was staring at her sent chills through her rodent body. She spun around to face her own human body standing across the hall, with chains around her wrists and ankles. *My God, I look so peaceful.*

She wanted to call for help, but all she could produce was a high-pitched squeak, which was mostly absorbed by the glass cage she was trapped in.

The past several weeks had been a wild roller coaster of emotions, topped by a sprinkle of pain. This was the third time that Sofia had found herself captured. This time hurt the most, however, because it came at the hands of someone she had trusted. *Everything and everyone in this land has some secret agenda.*

Sofia stood on her hind legs, sniffing the top of the enclosure and searching for weak points. Even if she managed to escape the box and return to her human self, she would still be trapped with no way out. But if Queen Prima killed her in her mouse form and destroyed all the magic paper, Sofia would never be able to return to her human self.

The only good thing she had going for her was that she had hidden the magic paper and the Knife of Life at Bartholomeu's.

She knew she could not count on Dalia to rescue her or for Roderick to swoop in like a superhero because he was probably somewhere being tortured. Or, even worse, he could be dead.

The hall that she found herself in was grand, to say the least. It was larger than the mirror hall in the Castle of Madness. A throne stood proudly on thc other end of the hall. A narrow red carpet stretched from the bottom of the throne to the large entrance door on the other end, with two royal guards standing at attention. The ceiling of the hall stretched out to the sky. Well, at least it looked that way from Sofia's perspective.

As she was taking in her surroundings, a loud thud returned her attention to the entrance door. She flinched at the sight of Queen Prima walking in, her dark satin dress fluttering freely behind her. An impressive tall crown made of dark thallium sat firmly on her head, complementing her pale face. The crown produced a darker shade of blue radiance, almost black. The queen carried a box similar to the one Sofia kept her paper origami in.

Sofia spun in a circle, shivering.

"Well, well, well . . . we finally meet after all these years," Queen Prima said, her words echoing through the grand hall. "Look at my little sister. And when I say little, I mean little." Queen Prima laughed as she kneeled on the floor in front of Sofia's mouse enclosure.

Sofia looked at Prima's joyful face and then at the engravings on the box she held tightly. Edgar's words found their way back to her thoughts. "*The Bracelet of Death contains a dragon, a basilisk, a gargoyle, a Dyoclon, a griffin, a spider, and a harpy.*"

The queen was more terrifying from this perspective than Sofia had imagined. She knew she was unable to hold a conversation with her in mouse form, and she preferred it that way, as she would not know what to say to her.

"I love family reunions, but they always turn out short and deadly." Prima laughed. Then she reached for the glass box, opened it from the top, and grabbed Sofia by the tail. She squeezed Sofia's tail tight. Prima carried her across the hall and toward her human body. She placed the mouse onto Sofia's palm, transforming the mouse into its paper shape. Then Prima seized the paper mouse and pulled her hand away from Sofia's.

Sofia gasped for air as life returned to her human host.

"You look so . . . beautiful," Prima said as she caressed Sofia's cheek. Sofia flinched.

"No need to be afraid, Sister."

Though Sofia doubted Prima's assurance, she had no other choice but to play the part. It did not matter what she said, as Prima would not believe her. Sofia would not believe herself if she was in Prima's shoes. Begging for her life would only make her more pathetic and desperate.

"What's wrong, little sister?" the queen spoke.

Sofia's body stiffened as words finally rushed out. "What did you do to Roderick?"

Prima frowned. "How cute, little sister. I am impressed, I have to admit. I thought you would beg for your life. Instead, you ask about a boy. He's not even your family."

“Family!” Sofia gasped as she clenched her fists. “How dare you speak of family? Are you talking about the same family you tortured and slaughtered?”

Prima stared at her for several seconds before she burst out laughing.

As Prima tried to compose herself, Sofia processed her escape options. *Who am I kidding? Without Roderick and Dalia by my side, I’m incapable of doing anything. I always have to rely on someone else’s help to get me out of trouble.*

But that’s not entirely true, her inner self said. *You solved the mystery of the cave on Cratos all by yourself.*

Yes, but only after Roderick saved me from falling to my death.

What about the Castle of Madness? That was some brilliant work on your part.

Are you kidding? That was not a work of brilliance. I was lucky, frustrated, tired, and afraid. That was an act of desperation.

What about the battle on Stanislas Hollow’s ship? You saved Dalia and single-handedly defeated the entire pirate force. Or saving Roderick from certain death at Bartholomeu’s?

I wish I’d never saved her.

“You are right,” Prima said, snapping Sofia out of her inner thoughts. “I can’t say I was ever happy to have a sister,” Prima said, moving her right hand to the top of the wooden box. “The moment you were born, everyone only talked about you. No one cared about the older sister anymore. *Elan this, Elan that*. Regardless, I learned to coexist. I used to play with you and take you for strolls around the castle. For a short moment, I was even happy to have a sister.

"Then, after all I did for you, you had to steal the one thing from me that I wanted the most—the Bracelet of Life. In retrospect, I am glad you did what you did because now I'm stronger than I ever was. I'm finally respected. I'm the Queen of Thalia."

Sofia looked at Prima, who was clearly consumed by her narcissism. Her hatred for Sofia was unmatched, incomprehensible. She could not believe how one sister could hate another so much. Her—Elan's—only sin was being born.

Sofia swallowed hard. "I feel sorry for the way you feel about me," she murmured. "It doesn't matter what I say, it will not make any sense to you. But I was a baby when the Bracelet of Life chose me. I wasn't the one who stole it from you. The Bracelet of Life chose me the same way the Bracelet of Death chose you. I did not want any of this to happen to you, to us."

"Stop with the rubbish I-love-you-sister-and-this-is-not-what-I-want story," Prima fired back. "You still took something from me, and that's the fact. You are responsible for all that happened to me, to our family, to the people of Thalia."

Sofia understood there was no reasoning with Prima, but she continued conversing with her, hoping to find a solution for a more pressing matter. How to escape from these shackles and from the castle.

"Did you ever ask yourself if you were born with this hatred? Do you hate me for being your sister, or do you hate the notion of having a sister?"

Prima's lips curled and her jaw clenched. "Don't you even think about playing these mental games with me." Prima opened the box in her hands and revealed seven paper creatures.

Sofia jerked back in her shackles. An army of terrifying creatures rose out of the box and assembled behind Prima.

Growls, screeches, and howls filled the room. The sight of a dragon, a gargoyle, and the other creatures that Prima had awoken made Sofia cringe. She wanted to hide, but there was no way to leave the tight grip of the metal shackles encompassing her wrists and ankles.

What made this sight even more terrifying was seeing Prima standing in the middle of the gang of dark creatures, smiling at Sofia, proud of her accomplishments. Prima's grip on dark magic was remarkable. Sofia was in a different league when it came to controlling her magic. She could admire the view as much as she feared it. *She is conscious and can control all her creatures at the same time.*

What was I thinking coming here in the first place? I never stood a chance.

Prima approached Sofia with renewed conviction, angrier than moments before. She moved into her face so Sofia could hear her words over the noise of the unruly creatures behind her. "You seem surprised, little sister. You clearly didn't expect me to be this powerful.

"Dalia Swiftblade kept me up to date on your travels and the progress of your magic. This entire time, I was miles ahead of you."

Anger flared in Sofia. *That backstabber. I can't believe she sold me for a bag of gold. What did I expect? To find a friend?*

"You never stood a chance, little sister. Never. And soon, you will join the rest of our family. Soon, I will finally be able to put an end to this, once and for all." Prima laughed. "I will make a spectacle of your death for the masses so that I can instill fear and dominance over their pitiful souls. You are the icing on the cake, little sister."

Sofia wanted to scream in anger but no sound left her mouth. Now, more than ever, she tried to wake up from this dream, from this nightmare. She would do anything right now to sit in a psychiatrist's office or at school. Sadly, she knew that would not happen.

She questioned her whole existence; what was real and what was not. Could it be that everything she had ever thought was real was fake, a dream? Had Edgar told the truth about her life?

"I have a little gift for you, little sister," Prima said, interrupting Sofia's thoughts. She snapped her fingers, and two of her guards left their positions along the walkway. They returned in seconds, pushing a man in front of them, a hood covering his head.

"Remove the hood!" Prima yelled.

As the hood came off, Sofia screamed. "No!"

She stared at Edgar. His face was swollen and bruised. One of the guards elbowed him on the back, sending his frail body to the floor.

A thick fabric covered his mouth, and his fragile hands were bound together before him. His eyes connected with Sofia's as he mumbled something from the ground that she was unable to decipher.

"I wanted to let you know that I got all your friends together," Prima announced. "It's like a little reunion. I wanted to do this in person to show you how excited I am to have you back, little sister." Prima waved her hands. The two guards moved away from Edgar, leaving him alone in the middle of the grand hall.

Prima looked up and closed her eyes for a moment; a smirk appeared on her face. Dyoclon, a dark, four-legged creature with a tail stretching more than six feet behind its muscular body and bleached teeth stretching past its elongated chin, approached Edgar. At the tip of the tail was a poisonous red stinger that glowed in the darkness of the hall. Dyoclon swung the tail, lodging its poisonous stinger through Edgar's heart. Edgar gasped as blood spilled over the marble floor of the great hall.

"How fitting," Queen Prima said as she smiled at Sofia.

"You monster!" Sofia screamed, clenching her fists. "You will pay for this, I promise you. You will pay for every person you killed, for every home you destroyed, for every dream you shattered. You are what you are because of the magic, but without it, you are one big nothing."

Sofia's attitude surprised and enraged Prima. She took the paper mouse she kept in her palm and approached Sofia. The warmth of Prima's breath engulfed Sofia's face with how close she was.

"You listen to me carefully. I will now send you back into your mouse body, little sister. I want you to feel as vulnerable and as useless as I felt on the day of the ceremony when you took what was mine. I wish a paper worm was an option so that you could look at yourself from its perspective. I want you to suffer and be unable to do anything about it." Prima forced the paper mouse into Sofia's right palm, transforming her into the mouse. Then she grabbed the mouse by the tail, making it squeak.

Prima threw Sofia back into the glass enclosure. Then she walked over to a tray a short distance away and picked up a small piece of cheese. She threw the cheese into the box with Sofia. "Listen to me carefully, little sister. I have your friend, Roderick, imprisoned, and he is being tortured as we speak. You can find yourself out of this box by eating that piece of cheese. The catch is that you only eat the cheese when you are ready to give up the location of where you hid the magic paper and the Knife of Life. As an incentive for your cooperation, I will stop torturing Roderick before his execution.

"I will leave poor Edgar's body for you as a reminder of what will happen to Roderick if you don't speak."

Prima turned around from the glass enclosure and approached Sofia's human body. She ran her hand through her blonde hair as she spoke her final words. "Sweet dreams, little sister."

****

Dalia sat on the prow of her ship, looking toward the horizon. Something wet snaked down her cheeks. She looked up into the sky, but no rain was falling.

"I am a traitor, and this is how everyone will treat me from now on," Dalia mumbled under her breath. She brushed tears from her cheeks as her vision blurred. More tears readied themselves. She gasped for fresh air when a cold, sharp object connected with her throat.

"If you make even the slightest move or release even the slightest sound, I will slit your throat like a loaf of bread," someone whispered from behind her.

Dalia gulped as three men climbed up onto the ship in front of her. One of the men was Hazard, the long-haired soldier from the City of Bones. He approached Dalia and then kneeled in front of her so he could face her eye-to-eye.

"I knew there was something about you, some hidden agenda. I'm glad I followed you here, scum," Hazard said, clenching his teeth afterward. "Before I kill you, you will help us rescue the princess."

Dalia did not try to fight. Her fighting flame had gone out when she had made a deal with the queen. Now, her only way out of this predicament was to help Hazard rescue the person she had betrayed.

CHAPTER 23

The sound of ceramic shattering resonated through the Pride cabin on Rainbow Lake.

Sofia dropped a piece of crusty bread as she spun her head instinctively. "My God, Mom. You scared me."

"Sorry, honey, I got a little distracted," her mother said, grinning.

"Hon, do you need any help?" her father volunteered as he walked into the room.

"I'll be fine; thanks for offering," her mother answered. She focused on gathering the broken dish from the farmer's sink. "Why don't you two clean up the yard while I deal with this mess?"

She did not have to repeat herself. Sofia and her dad found themselves outside the cabin before her mother could change her mind.

The sun had started to set on the horizon. The portable generator rattled in the background, drowning out the chirping birds nearby.

"Dad," Sofia said, holding a piece of uneaten bread in her hand, "want to feed the ducks?"

He smiled but did not offer an answer because he did not need to. Just by the sheer size of his smile, Sofia knew what his answer was.

The two of them ran toward the lakeshore.

"You know I'm not trying to compete with you, pumpkin!" her father yelled, his voice shaking from the short run.

"Sure, Dad," Sofia said as she came to a stop on the sandy shore.

The lake was situated about five hundred feet from the Pride cabin. The sky above the lake appeared to be bleeding red. The redness of the sky transferred onto the surface of the water below. The trees surrounding the lake had already exchanged their green clothes with all sorts of reds and browns. *Ah ... Autumn in Maine. There is nothing more beautiful than when the leaves start changing colors.*

As she gazed over the bleeding lake, a sound of quacking got her attention. She looked to her left to catch a glimpse of a column of ducks parading in her direction. She kneeled, mesmerized by the cuteness of the incoming duck train. She then looked down at her hand, clutching the bread. Sofia squeezed the bread, making small crumbs fall onto the sandy shore in front of her. The ducks quickly broke off their parading formation, wobbling toward the bread crumbs peppering the sand in front of them.

Her father slowly moved closer to her, walking on his toes, trying hard not to scare the incoming ducks. He kneeled next to Sofia, putting one arm around her shoulders. Their cheeks connected instinctively as the ducks vacuumed everything in their way.

"Honey," he said, turning toward Sofia, "promise me one thing."

Sofia looked at him with wondering eyes. "What's that, Dad?"

"Promise me that you will never forget me and your mom, that you will always cherish all of this, regardless of what you learn or hear about us."

Sofia frowned as she stared at her father. "I … I don't understand. What do you mean by that?" she stuttered.

"This here," he said, pausing for a moment to look around. "Your mom, myself … it's not what you think it is. It's hard to explain, but you will soon learn the truth. You will understand." Tears started to fill up in his eyes as he stared at Sofia. "You will always be my honey bee, regardless of what you deem real or imaginary. I will always love you from the bottom of my heart."

Sofia stared into her father's eyes, searching for something to make her understand his rambling. Moments later, his smile engraved itself into Sofia's pupils, which then slowly turned into blurriness. His face started to dissipate before her eyes. She tried to shake the feeling off, looking for clarity, but all her attempts were futile.

Now her father's face turned into the outline of another person, a different person. Sofia shut her eyes, not believing what was happening. She took a deep breath and then opened her eyes again. Her eyes widened as far as they could go as she stared at a demon—a demon bearing Dalia's face.

SNEAK PEEK IN BOOK 2

Sixteen Years Ago…

The Grand Witch sat strapped to a cold, metal chair, surrounded by bare and moldy concrete walls. She took a deep breath. However, the humidity almost choked her. She tried turning to either side, but a line of sharp needles attached to her head stopped her. She took several labored breaths in quick succession, managing to get just enough air into her lungs to feel alive again. Several deeper breaths followed as the air pushed through her veins until it reached her brain, clearing the blurred vision that unwillingly nested in her eyes.

The Grand Witch closed her eyes for a moment, looking for a piece of serenity in this unwelcoming place. Before she could find what she was looking for, though, the loud bang of a metal door from behind took her away from her endeavor.

Multiple pairs of feet walked into the room, but only one pair appeared before her—a royal soldier of impressive stature with a neatly pressed uniform and a handful of medals resting on his chest. It took a moment before the Grand Witch could put a name to the soldier's face.

Commander Trax of the Royal Guard.

ABOUT THE AUTHOR

Andjelko Napijalo resides in Maine with his wife, Sanela, and their dog, Sara. He is an avid hiker, runner, reader, and traveler. He gets his writing inspiration by traveling the world. *Soul Shifter* is Andjelko's debut novel.

Follow Andjelko Napijalo on Facebook and Instagram.
https://www.facebook.com/Andjelko-Napijalo-110975970729073

https://www.instagram.com/andjelkonapijalo/

www.ingramcontent.com/pod-product-compliance
Lightning Source LLC
Chambersburg PA
CBHW030519310726
48979CB00010B/1732/J
* 9 7 8 1 7 3 5 6 9 8 5 2 6 *